'Be grateful that fate intervened tonight, *cara*. I am not the man for you. You are curiously innocent, but there is a blackness in my soul that I fear would destroy you.'

Salvatore dropped a hard kiss onto her mouth and his gut clenched when he felt her immediate response. He closed his eyes briefly and thrust her away from him.

'Get out. Run from me, Darcey. Because if you don't I will take your lovely body and crush your gentle heart.'

His eyes glittered when she did not move and he hauled himself to his feet. Pain seared through his leg and he staggered against the bureau.

'Did you hear me?' he snarled. 'If you know what's good for you—get out!'

THE BOND OF BROTHERS

Bound by blood, separated by secrets

Dark, powerful and devastatingly handsome,
the Castellano brothers have fought much to overcome
their difficult childhood—but separation and secrets
have left their scars.

Now these two men must ensure that their children
do not inherit their painful legacy…

You read Sergio's story in:
HIS UNEXPECTED LEGACY
September 2013

Read Salvatore's story in:
SECRETS OF A POWERFUL MAN
November 2013

SECRETS OF A POWERFUL MAN

BY
CHANTELLE SHAW

MILLS
BOON

First published in Great Britain 2013
by Mills & Boon, an imprint of Harlequin (UK) Limited.
Harlequin (UK) Limited, Eton House, 18-24 Paradise Road,
Richmond, Surrey TW9 1SR

© Chantelle Shaw 2013

ISBN: 978 0 263 90060 6

Chantelle Shaw lives on the Kent coast, five minutes from the sea, and does much of her thinking about the characters in her books while walking on the beach. An avid reader from an early age, she found school friends used to hide their books when she visited—but Chantelle would retreat into her own world, and still writes stories in her head all the time.

Chantelle has been blissfully married to her own tall, dark and very patient hero for over twenty years and has six children. She began to read Mills & Boon® romances as a teenager, and throughout the years of being a stay-at-home mum to her brood found romantic fiction helped her to stay sane! Her aim is to write books that provide an element of escapism, fun, and of course romance for the countless women who juggle work and home life and who need their precious moments of 'me' time. She enjoys reading and writing about strong-willed, feisty women and even stronger-willed, sexy heroes. Chantelle is at her happiest when writing. She is particularly inspired while cooking dinner, which unfortunately results in a lot of culinary disasters! She also loves gardening, taking her very badly behaved terrier for walks and eating chocolate (followed by more walking—at least the dog is slim!).

Recent titles by the same author:

HIS UNEXPECTED LEGACY *(The Bond of Brothers)*
CAPTIVE IN HIS CASTLE
AT DANTE'S SERVICE
THE GREEK'S ACQUISITION

CHAPTER ONE

'THERE'S SOMEONE HERE to see you. A man...'

Darcey looked up from her desk, surprised that her usually unflappable secretary sounded flustered.

'He says his name is Salvatore Castellano,' Sue continued. 'He has been referred to you by James Forbes and wishes to arrange speech therapy for his daughter.'

'But James knows that the unit is closing.' Darcey was puzzled. James Forbes was head of the paediatric cochlear implant programme at the hospital and he had been vociferous in his condemnation of the financial cuts affecting the speech therapy unit.

Sue shrugged. 'I explained that, but Mr Castellano is insistent that he wants to see you.' She added in a conspiratorial voice, 'I think he's used to getting his own way, and he is demanding to speak to you. He's very *Mediterranean*—you know the type... Dark and intense. I know I shouldn't say this when I've been married to Brian for twenty-four years, but he's *hot*.'

He was *demanding* to see her? Darcey's brows rose, but she had to admit she was intrigued by this man who was responsible for turning Sue into a wilting heap of hormones. Fortunately she had no concerns that he might have the same effect on her. She was off hot men. From now on she would be perfectly happy with lukewarm and safe, perhaps even slightly boring, but definitely not a showman…like her ex-husband.

She glanced out of the window and noticed a sleek black saloon car parked next to her Mini. Her contract with the health authority had been terminated and she did not have to meet this Salvatore Castellano. But what the hell? There was only an empty house waiting for her, and a solitary dinner—if she could be bothered to cook.

'You'd better show him in.'

Sue stepped back into the corridor and Darcey returned to the task of clearing the drawers in her desk. The filing cabinets had been emptied and all that remained to do was take down the certificates on the wall which gave details of her qualifications: BSc (Hons), MSc in Speech and Language Therapy and an Advanced Clinical Skills Diploma for speech and language therapists to work with the deaf.

It was a pity that being an expert in her field had not been enough to save her job, she thought ruefully. The Inner London health authority's budget had been drastically cut and she had been made redundant. Losing her job had forced her to think about her future—and acknowledge the necessity of coming to terms with her past. Her decision to take a career break for a couple of months over the summer was primarily so that she could make plans for the private practice she intended to set up. But, more importantly, she was hoping to put her divorce behind her and get over her cheating rat of an ex-husband once and for all.

Her gaze fell on the nameplate on her desk. She had become Darcey Rivers when she had married Marcus and had kept his name after the divorce because she was reluctant to revert back to her maiden name and the notoriety that went with it. It had been painfully humiliating when she had realised that Marcus had married her because he had hoped that joining the famous theatrical Hart family would boost his acting career. Unfortunately she had been so in love with him, so bowled over by his wit and charm and undeniable good looks, that with uncharacteristic impulsiveness she had accepted his proposal four months after they'd met.

Darcey walked over to the window and picked up the potted plant on the sill. She had inherited the Maidenhair Fern two years ago, when she had taken up the post of senior specialist speech and language therapist. It had been half-dead and Sue had offered to throw it out—apparently this type of fern was notoriously difficult to grow successfully. But Darcey liked a challenge, and under her care the plant had thrived and was now a mass of bright green lacy leaves.

'Don't worry, I'll take you home with me,' she murmured. She had read that plants responded if you talked to them, and her words of encouragement seemed to have worked—although that was strictly between her and the fern. After all, she was a highly educated professional and *sensible* was her middle name; her family and friends would be astonished if they knew that she talked to plants.

The office door opened again, and she turned her head to see Sue usher a man into the room. Sunlight streamed through the window and danced across his rugged features. Darcey's first thought was that he was nothing like Marcus. But neither was he lukewarm, and he was definitely not safe. Now she understood what Sue had meant when she had said he was hot!

He looked as though he belonged to another century, when knights on horseback had fought bloody battles and rescued damsels in distress. Startled by the wild ex-

cesses of her imagination, Darcey forced herself to study
him objectively, but the image of an ancient king still remained in her mind. Perhaps it was the dangerously sexy
combination of black jeans and shirt and the well-worn
leather jacket that emphasised the width of his shoulders.
His height was equally impressive; the top of his head
brushed the door frame and she estimated that he must
be several inches over six feet tall.

Her heart gave a jolt as she raised her eyes to his face.
He was not conventionally handsome like Marcus. Not a
pretty boy. He was a man in the most masculine sense:
hard-faced, square-jawed, with a strong nose and dark,
penetrating eyes beneath heavy brows. His eyes gave
away nothing of his thoughts and his mouth was set in
an uncompromising line, as if he rarely smiled. His hair
was thick and so dark it was almost black, falling to his
shoulders. Darcey had a feeling that he cared little about
his appearance and had no inclination to visit a barber.

As she stared at him she was aware of a coiling sensation in the pit of her stomach. The feeling was entirely
sexual and utterly unexpected. She had felt dead inside
since she had discovered that Marcus was sleeping with
a glamour model with pneumatic breasts. The lightning
bolt of desire that shot through her now was so intense it
made her catch her breath. She sensed the power of the
stranger's formidable physique and for the first time in
her life acknowledged the fundamental difference between a man and a woman—male strength and feminine weakness.

She suddenly realised that she was holding her breath
and released it on a shaky sigh. Somehow she managed
to regain her composure and gave Salvatore Castellano
a polite smile.

'Mr Castellano? How can I help you?'

He glanced at the nameplate on her desk and frowned. 'Are *you* Darcey Rivers?'

He spoke with a strong accent. Italian, Darcey guessed. There was an arrogance about him that set her on the defensive.

'Yes, I am,' she said coolly.

He looked unimpressed. 'I expected someone older.'

James Forbes had said that Darcey Rivers was an experienced and dedicated senior speech therapist. The description had put into Salvatore's mind an image of a grey-haired, professional-looking woman, possibly wearing a tweed suit and spectacles. Instead he was faced with a slip of a girl with a heart-shaped face and a sleek bob of conker-brown hair that gleamed like silk in the bright sunlight pouring through the window.

He skimmed his eyes over her petite figure, noting how her fitted suit, reminiscent of the style worn in the 1940s, emphasised her tiny waist and the gentle flare of her hips. Her legs were slender and he guessed she chose to wear three-inch stiletto heels to make her appear taller. Her face was pretty rather than beautiful; her mouth was too wide and her eyes too big for her small features, giving her an elfin quality. Beneath her jacket her blouse was buttoned up to her neck and he briefly wondered if she was as prim as her appearance suggested.

Darcey flushed beneath the stranger's intent appraisal. 'I'm sorry if I've disappointed you,' she said with heavy irony.

'I am not disappointed, Miss Rivers.'

His voice was deep-timbred, with a sensual huskiness that made the hairs on the back of Darcey's neck stand on end.

'I am merely surprised. You seem young to be so highly qualified.'

Darcey knew she looked a good five years less than her age. Perhaps when she reached fifty she would be glad to look younger, but at university and at job interviews she had struggled to be taken seriously. Of course her name had not helped. Once people realised she was a member of the famous Hart family they were surprised that she had not followed her parents onto the stage. At least Salvatore Castellano was unaware of her family connection. But she felt irritated that he had mentioned her youthful appearance.

'I'm twenty-eight,' she told him tightly. 'And Rivers is my married name.'

His expression was inscrutable, 'My apologies, *Mrs* Rivers.'

Why on earth had she said that? Darcey asked herself. Intimating that she was married had been a subconscious response to his comment that she looked young. 'Actually, I prefer Ms Rivers.'

His shuttered expression did not alter, but she had an unsettling feeling that his dark eyes could see inside her head. Sue had gone, and he closed the door with a decisive click and walked across the office.

'I'm glad we've got that settled,' he murmured drily. 'Now, perhaps we can sit down and I will explain the reason for my visit?'

His arrogance was infuriating. Twin spots of colour flared on Darcey's cheeks and she had half a mind to tell him to get lost, but she hesitated when she noticed that he walked with a pronounced limp.

'A fractured femur—the result of a car accident,' he said curtly. 'My leg is held together with a lot of fancy metalwork.'

She was embarrassed that he had caught her staring at him. He made her feel as if she was sixteen again, immature and unsure of herself, lacking the self-confidence that the other members of her family possessed.

'Don't act like a timid mouse, darling girl,' had been her father's regular refrain. 'Project yourself to the audience and believe in yourself—because if you don't how can you expect anyone else to?'

It was all very well for her father, Darcey had often thought. Joshua Hart had earned a reputation as one of the finest Shakespearian actors in a career that had spanned three decades. Charismatic, exciting and unpredictable, he could also be distant with his children when he was focused on an acting role. As well as being an actor he was a brilliant playwright, and three of his plays had been performed in the West End. The one thing Joshua Hart certainly did not lack was self-belief.

'Acting is in your blood,' he'd often told Darcey. 'How could it not be, with the combination of genes you have inherited from your mother and me?'

Her mother, Claudia, was a gifted actress, and Darcey's brother and her two sisters had all followed their parents into the theatre. She was especially close to her younger sister Mina, and was proud of how she had overcome her disability to become a respected actress.

Only Darcey had chosen a different career path, and Joshua had not hidden his disappointment. Sometimes Darcey felt her father had taken her decision not to uphold the Hart family tradition and train at RADA as a personal affront. He had never been the easiest man to get on with, and in recent years she had sensed a divide between them that she longed to breach.

'Ms Rivers?'

Salvatore Castellano's curt voice snapped her back to the present. Without waiting for an invitation he pulled out the chair by her desk and sat down, stretching his injured leg stiffly out in front of him. Darcey decided that she needed to take control of the situation.

'I'm afraid I can only spare you a few minutes, Mr Castellano,' she said briskly. 'I have a busy afternoon.'

His brows rose. 'You mean you are holding appointments today? James Forbes led me to believe that the speech therapy unit has closed down.'

Flushing, because in actual fact she had nothing planned for the rest of the day, Darcey walked behind her desk and sat down, placing the potted fern in front of her like a barrier. 'So it has. I'm only here today to clear my office. Once I've finished I have...personal things to do.'

What kind of things? Salvatore wondered. Was she going home to her husband? Maybe to spend a lazy summer's afternoon making love? Glancing at her left hand, he was intrigued to see she was not wearing a wedding ring. He frowned. Ms Darcey Rivers's private life was of no interest to him. All he was interested in was her professional expertise.

'I have come to see you, Ms Rivers, because I wish to employ a speech therapist who specialises in working with deaf children, and specifically children who have cochlear implants,' he said abruptly. 'My five-year-old daughter had bilateral implants fitted two months ago. Rosa is profoundly deaf. She communicates using sign language but she has no audio-language skills.'

Darcey breathed in the subtle tang of his sandalwood cologne and a quiver of awareness shot through her. She wished now that she had not sat down at her desk, because rather than giving her a sense of authority all she could think was that, close up, Salvatore Castellano was devastatingly sexy.

For heaven's sake! She gave herself a mental shake and

concentrated on what he had told her. 'Did your daughter have the implants fitted in England?'

'Yes. James Forbes is her audiologist.'

'Then James must have explained that although the unit here is closing the speech therapy programme will still continue at the hospital, but on a smaller scale and with fewer therapists—which unfortunately will probably mean a longer waiting list before children can be assessed,' she said ruefully.

'James treated Rosa as a private patient. She does not qualify for the post-implant speech therapy programme provided by your National Health Service.'

'I see,' Darcey said slowly. 'In that case, why did James recommend me to you? Even if the speech therapy unit here wasn't closing, your daughter would not be eligible for me to assess her because I am employed—*was* employed,' she amended with a grimace, 'by the local health authority.'

'James said that you intend to establish a private practice.'

'I hope to do so in the future, but my immediate plans are to take a break from work and spend the summer in the South of France. I'm sorry I can't help you, Mr Castellano, but I can give you the names of several speech therapists who I'm sure would be willing to work with your daughter.'

Nothing on Salvatore Castellano's chiselled features indicated that he was disappointed by her response, but there was a steely implacability in his voice.

'James says you are the best in the business.' He speared Darcey with his penetrating stare. 'I want the absolute best for my daughter, and I am prepared to pay whatever fee you decide to charge for your expert knowledge.'

She frowned. 'It's not about money...'

'Experience has taught me that it is *always* about money, Ms Rivers.'

His sardonic reply riled her. Perhaps he thought that her decision to set up a private speech therapy practice had been made because she hoped to increase her earnings, as one of her ex-colleagues had suggested. But nothing could be further from the truth. What she wanted was more freedom to implement her own ideas and hopefully enhance hearing-impaired children's experiences of speech and language therapy. It was something Darcey cared passionately about, but she had a feeling that even if she tried to explain Salvatore Castellano would not understand.

She tried another approach. 'Obviously I can appreciate that you and Rosa's mother must be anxious for her to begin speech therapy as soon as possible. All the evidence shows that children with CI have the potential to achieve good communication and language skills if they receive therapy quickly after implantation.'

She hesitated, wondering where the child's mother was. It was strange that she was not with him. Alarm bells rang inside her head. She'd had past experience of parents who had not been in agreement over the type of help they wanted for their child.

'Can I assume that your daughter's mother agrees with your decision to employ a speech therapist?'

'My wife died when Rosa was a baby.'

Darcey shot him a startled glance, shocked by his revelation but even more so by the complete lack of emotion in his voice. 'I'm sorry,' she murmured. Her thoughts turned to his daughter. The little girl had been locked in a silent world for most of her life, and although she must be able to hear now that she had cochlear implants, sound must be a strange and perhaps frightening concept for her. Given that Rosa already had so much to cope with, the fact that she was growing up without her mother was desperately tragic—particularly as her father seemed as unemotional as a lump of granite.

Thoughts of her own mother flooded Darcey's mind. Six months ago Claudia had been diagnosed with a malignant melanoma. Luckily she had responded well to treatment, but Darcey remembered how devastated she had felt at the idea of losing her mum, and her heart ached for Salvatore Castellano's motherless little daughter.

She looked across the desk and found him watching her intently. From a distance his eyes had looked black, but now she saw that they were very dark brown, framed by thick black lashes. She wondered if his eyes became warmer when he smiled. Did he ever smile? Her gaze strayed to the stern line of his mouth. Would his lips soften if he kissed her? No doubt the dark stubble shading his jaw would graze her skin...

Snatching a sharp breath, she said quickly, 'I would like to help your daughter, Mr Castellano, but as I explained I will be out of the country for the next few months.'

'You are going to the French Riviera, I believe you said?'

'Yes. My family own a villa at Le Lavandou which I intend to use as a base. But I thought I might tour along the coast, maybe even drive into Italy.'

He gave her a speculative look. 'You speak as if you are going alone. Why isn't your husband going with you?'

It was on the tip of her tongue to tell him it was none of his damned business, but something in his expression made her drop her eyes from his piercing gaze.

'As a matter of fact I'm divorced,' she said stiffly.

'And there is no one else in your life? No boyfriend who is going to France with you?'

'I really don't see—'

'Because if that is the case,' he interrupted her, 'then there is no reason why you cannot spend the summer in Sicily and give my daughter the help she desperately needs. You mentioned you would like to visit Italy,' he reminded her. 'Sicily is the most beautiful part of Italy—although I admit I might be a little biased.'

The corners of his mouth lifted. It was not exactly a smile, but the hint that he wasn't completely made of ice, and even had a sense of humour, distracted Darcey's thought process.

'You're Sicilian?'

'To the depths of my soul.'

His accent was suddenly very strong. For the first time since he had walked into her office Darcey heard emotion in his voice, fierce pride in his heritage. 'I live in a castle that was built in the thirteenth century by one of my ancestors. Torre d'Aquila has been renovated and has all the facilities of a twenty-first-century home,' he said, mistaking her doubtful expression. 'You will be very comfortable. There is a private pool and the beach is nearby.'

She held up her hand. 'Mr Castellano, I'm sure your castle is lovely, but I haven't agreed to go to Sicily. For one thing I don't speak Italian, and I wouldn't be able to help Rosa learn her native language.'

'I have decided for several reasons that it will be better for her to learn English. My wife was half-English. Adriana died before Rosa was diagnosed as being profoundly deaf. I would like Rosa to learn her mother's language, and James Forbes thinks that now she can hear with the cochlear implants she might also be able to learn to speak Italian.'

Darcey nodded. 'I have met children with CI who are bilingual, but obviously it is important to concentrate on teaching Rosa one language to start with. I'm sure James has explained that, even though your daughter is now able to hear sound, developing language skills can be a slow process. She will need support and patience from her family as well as extensive speech therapy.'

'She is able to communicate using British sign language, which James tells me you are competent in.' Salvatore leaned across the desk and trapped Darcey's gaze. 'James spoke highly of your professionalism and skill, but more importantly, he said that you have a special empathy with deaf children.'

'My sister lost eighty percent of her hearing after she had meningitis when she was a child,' she explained. 'It was seeing how Mina struggled at first to cope with her deafness that made me decide that I wanted to work with hearing-impaired children.'

Salvatore heard the emotion in Darcey's voice and sensed she was softening. Determined to seize his advantage, he took his wallet from his jacket and pulled out a photograph of his daughter.

'Rosa is a shy child who, as a result of her disability, finds it hard to connect with people. I hope that the gift of language will help her self-confidence. I believe you can give her that gift, Darcey. James Forbes is confident that you are the best person to teach my daughter to speak.'

Oh, heavens! The way he said her name, in his gravelly, sexy accent, sent a little shiver down Darcey's spine. His dark eyes were mesmerising and his words tugged on her emotions. He was right, she thought. Language was a gift, but most people took the ability to hear and speak for granted. Darcey remembered how Mina had once confided that when she had lost her hearing she had felt lonely and isolated.

She studied the photo of a startlingly pretty little girl with a mass of dark curls framing a delicate face. Of course nothing in the photo revealed Rosa's deafness. Only when she looked closely did Darcey notice that there was no sparkle in the child's eyes but a sense of loneliness that was heart-wrenching.

It wouldn't hurt to see the child and make an assessment of her needs, Darcey mused. She could hand the case over to one of her colleagues who had also been made redundant and might be interested in working with Rosa.

Unbeknown to Darcey, her indecision was reflected in her eyes. She had beautiful eyes, Salvatore noticed. They were an unusual light green colour—the exact shade of the peridot pendant she was wearing suspended on a chain around her throat. He was surprised by the flicker of interest he felt. It was a long time since he had been intrigued by a woman. The delicate fragrance of her perfume—a sensual musk of jasmine and old-fashioned roses—teased his senses, and his eyes were drawn to the scattering of golden freckles on her nose and cheeks.

His mouth firmed as he reminded himself of the reason for his visit. His daughter needed the help of a speech therapist and Ms Rivers came with the highest recommendations. The fact that she was attractive was immaterial. There was no likelihood he would find her a distraction. During his lonely childhood he had learned to impose iron control over his feelings, and the loss of parts of his memory four years ago had only furthered his sense of emotional detachment.

'All I am asking at this stage is for you to visit my

house in London to meet Rosa,' he said. 'We can take things from there.'

Darcey chewed her bottom lip. 'It's not that I don't want to help your daughter, Mr Castellano—'

'Good,' he cut her off mid-sentence. 'I think the best thing would be for you to come and meet her now.' He got to his feet and towered over her, so that Darcey had to tilt her head to look at him. 'Can you postpone whatever plans you had for this afternoon?'

She wondered if he recognised the word *no*. He was like a steamroller, flattening any opposition to what he wanted, she thought ruefully. But she could not help but be impressed by his single-minded determination to help his daughter.

'I...I guess so.' Her cheeks grew pink as she recalled her white lie that she would be busy later. 'But I'm packed and ready to leave for France on Friday, so I don't really see the point.'

His dark eyes trapped her gaze. 'You would not say that if you were my daughter. Sadly, Rosa cannot say anything. She is unable to voice her thoughts, her hopes... her fears.'

He was deliberately playing on her emotions, Darcey recognised. But his ploy had worked.

She threw up her hands in surrender. 'All right, I'll come and meet your daughter. I'll assess the level of speech therapy she needs and then, if you wish, I will hand her case over to one of my colleagues. But I have to warn you, Mr Castellano, there is no chance I will go to Sicily with you.'

CHAPTER TWO

'I'LL TAKE MY car,' Darcey told Salvatore as they walked across the car park. Despite his injured leg his stride was twice the size of hers, and her stiletto heels tip-tapped on the tarmac as she tried to keep pace with him.

'There's no need for you to drive through the centre of London. I'll drop you back here later so that you can collect your car.'

She shook her head. 'I don't know you, Mr Castellano, and I'm not going to get into a stranger's car.'

Personal safety was an issue she took very seriously. Her parents also owned a touring theatre company and ran drama workshops in schools and youth clubs to promote ways for young people to stay safe. Before she had become involved in her own career Darcey had frequently performed with the company, Speak Out, which also promoted drama for the deaf community.

'I promise I have no plans to ravish you on the back seat,' Salvatore said drily.

He glanced at the petite woman at his side and idly wondered if the spark of fire in her green eyes would live up to its promise. Outwardly Darcey appeared cool and collected, but beneath her smart suit he sensed she was an explosive bundle of sexual energy.

He frowned, annoyed by his unexpected train of

thought. 'You are welcome to sit in the front with my chauffeur.'

Through the Bentley's smoked glass windows Darcey made out the figure of a driver sitting behind the wheel and she felt like an idiot.

'As for not knowing who I am,' Salvatore continued, 'do you drink wine?'

She gave him a puzzled look. 'Occasionally. My father is interested in fine wines and has built up a large collection.'

'Then he will almost certainly know that the wines from the Castellano Estate are the finest in Sicily.' Reaching inside his jacket, Salvatore withdrew a business card and handed it to her.

Darcey glanced at the logo on the card and recognition dawned.

'Castellano Wine! I've seen the label on wines in supermarkets and specialist wine shops. My father says the Castellano vineyards produce the best wine that has ever come from Sicily.' She looked uncertainly at Salvatore. 'So…do you work for the company?'

'I own it,' he said coolly. 'At least, I own the vineyards and the winery, and also a wine distribution business under the umbrella of the Castellano Group, which is a multi-faceted global organisation. My father retired from the company last year, leaving me and my twin brother as joint CEOs. Sergio is responsible for the property development division, and also has a personal interest in the Hotel Royale in Bayswater, which the company purchased and refurbished a couple of years ago.'

Salvatore opened the rear door of the Bentley.

'Now that you know as much about me as you need to know, will you accept my offer of a lift to my house in Mayfair?'

Darcey was still reeling from the realisation that he must be very wealthy—probably a multi-millionaire at the very least. Where else would he own a house but in the most expensive area of London? she thought wryly.

She shook her head. 'I'd still prefer to take my car.' It meant that she was in control and could leave his home when she chose.

Salvatore frowned. He was used to being obeyed without question, and he found Darcey's obstinacy irritating, but she was already getting into her car.

'I'll follow you,' she said, 'but you had better tell me your address and I'll put it into my sat nav.'

He gave her the postcode. 'It's on Park Lane, close to Marble Arch.' Salvatore snatched his eyes from the expanse of slender thigh exposed as Darcey's skirt rode up her legs as she climbed into her car and ruthlessly dismissed his faint stirring of sexual interest. 'It will be simpler for Rosa's sake if we drop formality and use our Christian names. Darcey is a charming name.'

Feeling hot and bothered by the predatory glint she had glimpsed in Salvatore's eyes, Darcey was glad of the distraction.

'It has both Irish and French origins. My father is half-Irish and half-French and he chose the name for me.'

'The meaning of Salvatore is saviour.'

To Darcey's surprise he gave a harsh laugh, and for a second she glimpsed a tortured expression in his eyes that was truly shocking.

His expression hardened and became unreadable once more. 'The irony isn't lost on me,' he muttered obliquely.

She wondered what he meant, but before she could ask he slid into the back of the Bentley and disappeared from view behind the darkened windows. He was a man of mystery and absolutely the last thing she needed when

she was two days away from her holiday, Darcey thought
as she started the Mini's engine and followed the Bentley
out of the car park. For weeks she had been daydream-
ing about relaxing on a golden beach, eating melting Brie
on crusty French bread, and drinking the local red wine.
She was regretting her impulsive decision to meet Salvatore's daughter, but as she recalled the photo of Rosa
she could not help feeling sympathetic towards the little
girl with the sad eyes.

Traffic in the capital at the start of the rush hour was
heavily congested, and Darcey had lost sight of the
Bentley by the time she crawled along Oxford Street
and turned onto Park Lane. Opposite was Marble Arch
and the green oasis of Hyde Park, but she was too busy
looking for the address Salvatore had given her to be able
to admire the famous London landmarks. Suddenly she
caught sight of the Bentley parked in front of a stunning
neo-classical style mansion house. Hastily indicating to
change lanes, she nipped into a parking space, thankful
that her small car was so easy to manoeuvre.

Salvatore was standing on the front steps of the house
and seemed to be in deep conversation with a striking
blonde wearing a very short skirt and a low-cut top that
revealed her enviable cleavage. Darcey sensed from their
body language that they were arguing. The woman spun
away from him, but he followed her down the steps and
caught hold of her arm.

Feeling awkward at the idea of interrupting a lovers'
tiff, Darcey remained in her car and watched the woman
jerk free from Salvatore and climb into a waiting taxi,
which immediately sped away. She was tempted to drive
off too, but he was striding along the pavement towards
her, his powerful masculinity in no way lessened by the

slight unevenness of his gait due to his injured leg. With a sigh, she got out of the Mini and went to meet him.

'It might be best if I left,' she said, feeling her heart skitter when he halted in front of her. Her reaction to him was all the more unsettling because she could not control it. Since her divorce eighteen months ago she had not felt the slightest interest in men, and she was horrified by her body's response to Salvatore's potent virility.

He frowned, and she explained, 'I saw you arguing with your girlfriend and I thought you might want to go after her.'

'That wasn't my girlfriend,' he said curtly, and Darcey suddenly realised that his temper was on a tight leash. 'Sharon was my daughter's nanny. I hired her through an agency when I brought Rosa to England for surgery to fit the cochlear implants. The arrangement was that Sharon would accompany me back to Sicily and continue looking after Rosa. But she has just informed me that she has got back together with a boyfriend and is moving to Birmingham to be with him.'

'So who is looking after Rosa now?'

'Sharon said she had asked one of the maids to keep an eye on her.'

Darcey could imagine how confused and upset Rosa must feel at being abandoned by the nanny who was supposed to be taking care of her. 'Poor little girl,' she said softly.

There was no flicker of emotion in Salvatore's dark eyes. 'Unfortunately Luisa—the nanny who had looked after Rosa since she was a baby—left to get married shortly before we came to England. Finding someone able to use sign language at short notice was difficult, and Sharon was the only person on the agency's books. I admit that when I took her on I was unaware of her boyfriend problems.' He glanced at Darcey. 'Come and meet my daughter.'

He began to walk back towards thc house, and after a moment's hesitation Darcey hurried after him. 'Was Rosa close to her previous nanny?'

He shrugged. 'I suppose so. My daughter has no memory of her mother and had only been cared for by Luisa. I imagine she missed her at first, but she's a resilient child.'

Darcey was chilled by his cool tone and his curiously detached air when he spoke about his little girl. She wondered if a five-year-old could really be as resilient as he seemed to think, but she made no comment as she followed him up the steps and into the house. With grey marble walls and floor, and elegant antique furniture, the entrance hall looked more like the foyer of a five-star hotel—with the same impersonal feel. It was obvious that expert interior designers had been given a limitless budget to spend, but although it was a beautiful house it was not a home, and seemed as cold and unwelcoming as its owner.

Darcey glanced at Salvatore's hard profile as they walked up the sweeping staircase. 'This is a stunning place,' she commented.

'Do you think so? There's rather too much marble decor for my taste, but I suppose it's impressive.' His tone was sardonic. 'My brother purchased the house to add to his property portfolio. When he married his English wife he considered using it as a London base, but he and Kristen have a very lively four-year-old son, and now another child on the way. They rarely visit England, so I bought the house from Sergio. Most of the time it is rented out to an Arab sheikh. I have only been staying here for the past couple of months, while Rosa had the cochlear implants fitted and adjusted.'

At the top of the stairs Salvatore led Darcey along the landing and opened a door. As she stepped into the room she noticed that a half-hearted attempt had been made to make the room child-friendly, with posters of fairies on the walls and a large dolls' house in the corner. A movement from over by the window caught her attention, and she watched a little girl slide down from the window seat and run across the room.

Rosa was tall for her age, and even prettier than the photo Darcey had seen of her. Her curly hair was tied in a ponytail, and her dark eyes, framed by long lashes, were hauntingly beautiful. A small earpiece attached to a wire that disappeared beneath her tee shirt and was attached to a battery pack was the only sign of her hearing impairment. Darcey knew that another wire running from the earpiece to a small circle taped to Rosa's head, was linked magnetically to the implant inside her skull, enabling her to hear.

Rosa's face had lit up at the sight of her father, but as she came towards Salvatore her steps slowed and she gave him an uncertain smile that made Darcey's heart ache. She expected Salvatore to sweep his daughter into his arms, but although he gave a brief smile he seemed strangely awkward and patted Rosa's head, as if he were a distant uncle who was unused to children.

Why don't you cuddle your daughter? Darcey wanted to ask him. He did not appear to notice the little flash of hurt in Rosa's eyes, but Darcey saw, and she felt a pang of sympathy for the child.

She recalled instances from her own childhood when she had felt rejected by her father. Joshua had never meant to be deliberately cruel, but he'd often been self-absorbed and careless of other people's feelings. As an adult Darcey understood his artistic temperament, but as a child she had been hurt and had believed that she had done something to upset her father.

She leaned down so that her face was level with Rosa's. 'Hello, Rosa. My name is Darcey,' she said gently, speaking the words at the same time as she signed them.

Hello, Rosa signed, but made no attempt to speak. She looked up at her father and asked in sign language, *Where is Sharon?*

Salvatore hesitated before he signed back: *She had to go and visit a friend.*

When is she coming back?

Another pause, and then he signed, *She isn't.*

Rosa's lip trembled. Darcey shot Salvatore a glance, willing him to lift his daughter into his arms and reassure her that, although the nanny had gone, he would never leave her.

But instead he signed, *Darcey has come to play with you.*

That's right—hand the problem over to someone else, she thought, flashing him a fulminating glare. She did not understand what was wrong with him. His determination to arrange speech therapy for Rosa suggested that he cared about the little girl, but he seemed incapable of expressing his emotions.

Perhaps he really was as hard as his granite-like features suggested and did not feel the normal range of emotions most people felt. Darcey could only guess what effect his detachment would have on his five-year-old daughter, who had to cope with deafness and was growing up without a mother. If any child needed her father's love it was Rosa, but Salvatore seemed to have a heart of stone.

'I will need to make a proper assessment to determine the level of speech therapy Rosa needs,' she told him. 'It should take an hour or so.' She frowned when he strode over to the door. 'I assumed you would want to be present during the assessment.'

'I'll leave you to get on with your job while I phone the agency and arrange a replacement for Sharon.' Salvatore saw no reason to explain that he was in a hurry to go to his study because he had just received a text message asking him to call his brother about an urgent matter.

'But—'

'Rosa will probably respond better if I'm not here,' he cut her off abruptly. He could tell from the glowering look Darcey gave him that she did not think him much of a father. Guilt clawed in his gut. She was right, he thought grimly. He was not the sort of father he wished he could be. The truth was he did not know how to act like a loving parent. When he had been growing up his father had been a remote figure. And as for his mother—well, the less said about her the better.

He had been five years old when Patti had left. He had never understood why she had forbidden him and his brother from calling her *mamma*. She had disappeared one day and taken Sergio with her. Salvatore had assumed she loved his twin and that was why she had taken him to America. It turned out that she had not loved Sergio either. Recently his brother had confided that Patti had been an alcoholic who had often beaten him when she'd had too much to drink.

Salvatore did not know if he felt better or worse now that his illusions about his mother had been shattered. For so many years he had put her on a pedestal and believed he was unworthy of being loved. That belief was still deeply ingrained on his psyche. Maybe it was why he found it so hard to show his emotions.

He wished things were different. He wished he could

be an openly loving *papa* to Rosa, like his brother, Sergio, was to his son, Nico. But always in the back of his mind was the guilt that it was his fault Rosa was growing up without her mother, the fear that one day she would learn the truth and perhaps would hate him.

He jerked his gaze from the accusatory expression in Darcey Rivers's bright green eyes. 'I will be in my study. Press nine on the phone if you need anything and a member of staff will attend to you.'

Salvatore barely glanced at Rosa as he exited the nursery, Darcey noticed. She could not understand his remoteness from his daughter. It seemed as though he preferred to hand over the little girl to a nanny, but now Sharon had left and Rosa had no one to take care of her.

She glanced at the child and her heart ached when she saw the wistful expression on her face. Smiling, she walked over to Rosa and crouched down beside her. *I like your dolls' house*, she signed. *Can I play too?*

Dark eyes studied her gravely for a few moments. Rosa had inherited her father's eyes, Darcey noticed. She tried to block out the image of Salvatore's ruggedly handsome face from her mind, annoyed by her inexplicable attraction to the cold and enigmatic man. She was here in her professional capacity, and she was determined to concentrate solely on the little girl who was smiling tentatively at her.

Over the next hour it quickly became clear that Rosa was a highly intelligent child, but although she was proficient in sign language she was unable or unwilling to attempt to speak. The little girl would need plenty of encouragement to develop self-confidence as well as to master language skills.

The nursery door opened and Darcey glanced over her

shoulder, expecting to see that Salvatore had returned.
But a butler stood in the doorway and informed her that
it was Rosa's dinner time.

'Mr Castellano is unavoidably detained and has asked
if you would accompany his daughter to the dining room.'

She could not refuse when Rosa slipped a small hand
into hers and gave her a trusting smile, and she was glad
she had stayed with the little girl when they walked into
the huge dining room. A single place was set at one end
of a long dining table.

Doesn't your father eat dinner with you? she signed
to Rosa.

The child shook he head. *Papa eats later. He is always busy in his office.*

Darcey felt another pang of sympathy for Salvatore's
little daughter, who was growing up in such isolated
splendour. Clearly she did not lack for material things,
but Darcey sensed that Rosa yearned for companion-
ship and love.

Will you stay and play with me? Rosa signed when
she had finished her meal.

Realising that there was no one else to take care of
her, Darcey decided she would have to stay with the little girl and wait for Salvatore. Back in the nursery, she
played a few more games with Rosa before helping her
to get ready for bed. Rosa removed the battery pack she
had worn during the day and the device behind her ear
that was the cochlear implant processor.

I don't like the dark, she signed when Darcey pulled
the curtains and was about to turn off the bedside lamp.
Will you leave the light on?

Recalling how Mina had hated the dark, because
she had felt cut off when she could neither see nor hear,
Darcey nodded. Rosa reminded her so much of her sis-

ter when they had been children. Perhaps that was why she felt an immediate bond with the little girl. But while Mina had grown up with the support of loving parents and family, Rosa had no one but her stern-faced father.

Darcey was appalled by Salvatore's seemingly uncaring attitude towards his daughter. He might be the sexiest man she had ever laid eyes on but beneath his devastating good looks he was as selfish as her ex-husband. It was about time someone told Salvatore Castellano a few home truths, she thought grimly.

Salvatore stared moodily out of his study window and noticed that the trees in Hyde Park opposite resembled black silhouettes in the gathering dusk. After he had spoken to his brother and learned that there had been a fire at the winery in Sicily he had been busy on the phone, dealing with the crisis, and had not realised how late it was. He felt guilty that he had left Rosa for so long, but the maid had reported that Darcey Rivers had stayed to help his daughter with her bedtime routine.

He grimaced. No doubt his absence had confirmed her belief that he was an uninterested father. The truth was far more complicated. He loved Rosa, but love was not something he'd had much experience of and he did not know how to get close to his child.

He closed his eyes, trying to control the searing pain in his head. The migraines that had plagued him since the accident four years ago had become more frequent in recent months, and were so debilitating that he was forced to resort to taking painkillers. It was no coincidence that this headache had started soon after he had spoken to Sergio and heard the shocking news his old friend Pietro was dead. The elderly vintner had suffered a fatal heart attack while trying to fight the blaze at the winery.

It was particularly poignant that Pietro had given his life for the wine that he was so proud of, he thought. Winemaking had been in Pietro Marelli's blood. A third generation vintner, with no son to pass his knowledge on to, he had instead shared his expertise with Salvatore. But, more than that, Pietro had been a substitute father who had welcomed a lonely boy into his home and his heart. Every school holiday Salvatore had returned to the Castellano estate and rushed to see Pietro first, knowing that Tito, his father, would be working in his office and would not welcome being disturbed.

It was strange that he could remember his childhood but had no memory of the accident, Salvatore brooded. He had a clear vision of himself as a ten-year-old boy, walking through the vineyards with Pietro to inspect the grapes, but no recollection of the events that had happened after he had got behind the wheel of his car and driven Adriana away from that party. All he remembered was waking to find he was in hospital and being told that his wife had been killed when their car had spun out of control on a mountain road and plunged over the edge.

The doctor had told Salvatore he had been lucky to escape with his life, albeit with a seriously mangled right leg and a head injury. It had caused no permanent brain damage. His amnesia, so the specialist suspected, was psychogenic. In layman's terms, his inability to remember the accident, or much of his marriage, was his brain's defence mechanism in order to blot out the grim fact that he was responsible for his wife's death.

Salvatore felt a familiar surge of frustration as he tried to cast his mind back in time and hit a wall of blackness. It seemed inconceivable that he could have married a woman, who had given birth to his child, and yet he had no recollection of their relationship. His mother-in-law had put photographs of Adriana everywhere in the castle, but when he looked at the pictures of his wife he felt no connection to her.

The specialist had told him it was likely his memory would eventually return, but until it did Salvatore felt he was trapped in a dark place, with no past and no future, unable to forgive himself for robbing his daughter of her mother.

He kneaded his throbbing temples with his fingers and thought about the rest of his conversation with his brother. Sergio had reported better news about the estate workers who had been burned in the fire. Their injuries were serious, but thankfully not life-threatening.

Hearing a tap on the study door, Salvatore turned his head and watched Darcey enter the room. Her silky copper-brown hair framed her face, and she had taken off her jacket. He could see the shape of her small, firm breasts beneath her blouse. His analytical brain registered that she was very attractive, but he was surprised by the bolt of awareness that shot through him. Earlier, in her office, he had ignored the sexual chemistry between them, but tonight, to his annoyance, his eyes were drawn to the curve of her mouth and he fleetingly imagined covering her soft lips with his.

None of his thoughts were revealed on his hard features, however. 'Is Rosa asleep?'

'Do you care?' Green eyes flashed fire at him. 'Your daughter went to bed forty minutes ago and stayed awake for ages, waiting for you come and wish her goodnight.'

'I apologise.' Salvatore's eyes narrowed on Darcey's furious face. 'I had to deal with an important matter.'

'It's not *me* you should apologise to. Rosa was disappointed when you didn't show up.' Darcey's mouth tightened. As she had watched Rosa struggling to stay awake she had recalled doing the same thing when she had been a child, waiting for her father to come home from the theatre. On the nights when Joshua had remembered to come up and kiss her goodnight she had fallen asleep feeling happy, but sometimes he'd forgotten and then she had cried herself to sleep.

Salvatore seemed to be unaware of how much his little girl needed him. Darcey glared at him, wishing she could ignore his potent masculinity. He had discarded his jacket and rolled up his shirtsleeves to reveal darkly tanned forearms covered with a mass of black hair. His brooding sensuality was dangerously attractive—but she wasn't looking for danger or excitement, wasn't looking for a man at all. And certainly not one who made her feel so acutely aware of her femininity.

'What could possibly be more important than your daughter?' she demanded. 'How could you have left her for several hours with a complete stranger?'

'You work with children in your professional capacity. I knew you would take care of her. The butler told me that Rosa seemed quite happy with you.'

His casual attitude inflamed Darcey's temper. 'So your butler is an expert in child psychology, is he?' she said sarcastically. 'You are *unbelievable*!'

She turned back to the door. It was none of her business that Salvatore was so distant from his daughter, she reminded herself. Rosa was a sweet little girl, but Darcey was *not* going to allow her soft heart to overrule her common sense, which was telling her she needed to walk out of this marble house and away from Salvatore Castellano and his sad-eyed little daughter.

'I can't believe your uncaring attitude to Rosa,' she said disgustedly. 'The poor little scrap doesn't have a mother and, to be frank, from what I've seen she doesn't have much of a father.'

Her words hit Salvatore as if she had physically slapped him, but he revealed no emotion on his chiselled features. He was not used to being criticised and was irritated that he felt the need to explain himself to Darcey.

'I usually visit Rosa to wish her goodnight, but I've already said that unfortunately I was detained this evening.'

'You were too busy working to spare a few minutes for a lonely little girl?' Darcey said scathingly, recalling how Rosa said that her father was always busy in his office.

Salvatore's jaw tightened. 'Earlier this afternoon there was a fire in one of the warehouses at my winery in Sicily. Hundreds of barrels of prized wine have been destroyed, but much worse than that, three of the estate workers were injured in the blaze. I have been making arrangements for the men to be flown to a specialist burns unit on mainland Italy and organising for their families to be with them. I had not forgotten about Rosa, but I admit I was so involved with the crisis at home that I did not realise how late it was.'

He raked a hand through his hair and Darcey noticed the lines of strain around his eyes. He hid his emotions well, but he was clearly concerned about the workers injured in the fire.

'The agency that sent Sharon does not have another nanny on their books who is able to use sign language, and I haven't had time to try a different agency.' His dark eyes sought Darcey's. 'But thank you for taking care of Rosa this evening. The least I can do is offer you dinner here with me tonight.'

'No, thank you. I have to go.'

The idea of spending another five minutes alone with Salvatore filled Darcey with panic. His explanation about why he had not come up to the nursery to see Rosa was understandable, but she still sensed that there were issues with his relationship with his daughter that she did not understand. She did not want to get involved with this enigmatic man whose seductively husky voice was causing her heart to beat too fast.

Without another word she hurried out of the study. Her jacket and laptop were on the chair in the hall, where she had left them, but as she walked over to them, with the intention of continuing out through the front door, Salvatore's voice stopped her.

'Can your conscience allow you to abandon Rosa?'

'*Me* abandon her?' She spun round and glared at him. 'That's rich, coming from her father—who can't be bothered to spend time with her and expects the staff to care for her. *My* conscience has nothing to worry about.'

As she uttered the words Darcey discovered that her conscience was far from happy. The image of Rosa's trusting expression when she had tucked her into bed tugged on her heart. She remembered how the little girl had signed that she was afraid of the dark. Many young children shared the same fear, but for a deaf child that feeling of isolation must be worse.

'I have left notes of my assessment on Rosa which you can pass to another speech therapist when you find one who is prepared to go to Sicily.'

'My daughter has already bonded with you.'

She tried to ignore the pull his words had on her emotions. 'I suppose your butler told you that?' she said sarcastically.

'No, I saw for myself that Rosa likes you.'

Salvatore hesitated and to Darcey's surprise a hint of emotion flickered across his face.

'I came to see her while she was eating her dinner. The two of you were laughing together...'

She gave him a puzzled look. 'Why didn't you join us?'

'Rosa looked like she was having fun, and I did not want to interrupt.'

The truth was he had felt jealous as he had watched his daughter interacting with Darcey, Salvatore acknowledged to himself. Rosa did not laugh very often—not with him, anyway. The only time she seemed truly happy was when she was playing with her cousin, Nico.

He wished he could breach the distance that existed between them. A distance he felt was widening as she grew older. Even though Rosa could now hear with the cochlear implants, he did not know how to reach his little girl. Deep in his heart he admitted that he found her deafness difficult to accept. In his darkest thoughts he wondered if he was to blame for her loss of hearing.

Why was he allowing his mind to dwell on the blackness within him? Salvatore asked himself. He was sure that Darcey's expertise would enable her to help Rosa learn to talk and, more than that, he felt instinctively that she would be able to connect with his daughter in a way he could not. When he had stood outside the dining room and watched her with Rosa he had been struck by her genuine kindness to his daughter. Somehow he had to persuade her to come to Sicily.

'Rosa needs you.'

Darcey hesitated, her indecision apparent on her expressive face. Salvatore sensed that she was close to giving in. He glanced towards the butler, who had stepped into the hall.

'The chef has prepared dinner for you and your guest, sir.'

The timing was perfect. 'Thank you, Melton. Ms Rivers and I will make our way to the dining room,' Salvatore said smoothly.

CHAPTER THREE

'It is my fault you were delayed tonight, and I feel bad at the thought of you driving home to cook a meal this late in the evening.' Salvatore forestalled the argument he could see Darcey was about to make. 'Also, my chef is French, and very temperamental. If he is upset he's likely to serve me frogs' legs for breakfast.'

Darcey chewed on her bottom lip, disconcerted by the revelation that Salvatore had a sense of humour. She was torn between wanting to leave, which was by far the most sensible option, and a wholly emotional response to his daughter, who aroused her sympathy.

While she dithered Salvatore opened the door to the dining room. 'Come and eat,' he invited.

His harsh tone had softened and the sensual warmth in his voice melted Darcey's resistance. Against her better judgement she followed him.

The moment she sat down at the table the butler appeared, to serve a first course of classic French *consommé*. The piquant aroma rising up from the bowl teased her tastebuds and her stomach gave a growl, reminding her that it was hours since she had eaten a sandwich for lunch.

The butler offered her wine, but knowing that she had to drive home she refused and opted for water. To her surprise, Salvatore did the same. She glanced at chiselled features that gave no clue to his thoughts and sensed that his mind was far away. He was not the most talkative host, she thought ruefully as she searched her mind for something to say to break the silence.

'Why did you choose to become a vintner?'

He shrugged. 'As a child I was drawn to the vineyards. I was fascinated to see the grapes swell on the vines and I wanted to understand the process by which they were turned into wine. I was lucky enough to have a good teacher.'

'Your father?'

'No.'

Salvatore saw that Darcey was surprised by his curt reply, but her questions had ripped open his heart and exposed the pain he had been trying avoid for the past hours. He did not have time to mourn for Pietro now. He would pay his respects to his old friend when he returned to Sicily. But for one of only a few times in his life his emotions threatened to overwhelm him and grief lay heavy in his heart. The painkillers he had taken had not kicked in yet, and his head throbbed. He wished he could be alone, but it was important that he secured Darcey Rivers's agreement to take the job as Rosa's speech therapist.

Truly, she had never met such a surly man as Salvatore, Darcey thought as she gave up trying to make conversation and finished her soup. She could see it was going to be hard work to persuade him to interact with his daughter.

It was a relief when the butler arrived to serve the main course of herb-crusted salmon and new potatoes. She picked up her knife and fork and realised that they were made of solid silver, to match the ornate candelabra standing in the centre of the table. Glancing around the sumptuous dining room, she found her attention caught by the painting on the wall that she had noticed when she had brought Rosa down to dinner earlier.

'That can't be an original Monet?' she murmured. She had recently read in a newspaper that one original Monet painting had sold for several million pounds.

Salvatore flicked a brief glance at the painting. 'It is.'

Darcey looked at him curiously. 'Are you interested in art?' An appreciation of art suggested that beneath his granite exterior he might actually be human.

'I am interested in artwork for its investment value.'

She grimaced. 'That's not what I meant. Are you only interested in things for their financial worth?'

'Money makes the world go round,' he said sardonically. 'And, speaking of money…' He slid a piece of paper across the table towards her. 'This is the amount I am prepared to pay if you will agree to come to Sicily.'

Her heart lurched as she stared at the figure scrawled on the cheque.

'I hope you will find the amount adequate recompense for forgoing your holiday. I thought the money would be useful for when you establish your private practice.'

'It certainly would be,' she said faintly. If she accepted the money she would not have to apply for a bank loan to set up her business, Darcey mused. Heck, she wouldn't have to work at all for a year. 'You must have a huge amount of faith that I will be able to help Rosa.'

Salvatore shrugged. 'I trust James Forbes's judgement that you are an excellent speech therapist, and of course I checked your qualifications before I made the decision to appoint you.'

Darcey stared at Salvatore's hard-boned face and felt chilled by his complete lack of emotion. It was no good telling herself that Rosa was not her problem. The lit-

tle girl needed her—just as her sister had needed her
help and support when Mina had struggled to cope with
her deafness. But Salvatore's arrogant assumption that
she would be impressed by his wealth infuriated her. He
was going to find out that, although he might be used to
flashing his money around to get whatever he wanted,
he could not buy *her*.

'You have no idea, do you?' she said as she tore up
the cheque and pushed the pieces back across the table.

Salvatore's eyes narrowed. Why had he thought that
Darcey might be different from the countless other
women he had met who were seduced by his wealth? he
asked himself derisively. Clearly she was out to get what
she could, and having recognised an original Monet on
the wall had decided to push for more.

'Is it not enough money?' he demanded curtly.

'It's an *obscene* amount of money.'

He frowned. 'I don't understand.'

'I know—and that's the saddest part. You think money
can buy you anything you want. But money won't help
your daughter learn to speak. Rosa needs time, patience
and support—and not only from a speech therapist,'
Darcey said, guessing what Salvatore was about to say.
'She needs those things from *you*.'

Darcey stared at Salvatore's shuttered expression
and despaired of making him understand how vital his
input would be with his daughter's therapy. With a re-
signed sigh she mentally waved goodbye to her holiday
in France. Her conscience would not allow her to abandon Rosa.

'I have decided to go Sicily with you.' She saw a flash
of surprise cross his hard features as he glanced at the
torn up cheque. She continued crisply, 'My fee will be
the same as the monthly salary I was paid by the health

authority. I don't want any more than that. I am prepared to stay at your castle and give Rosa intensive speech therapy for three months, during which time I will help you to find another therapist who can provide her with long-term support. I have to be back in London at the end of September. That's non-negotiable,' she added, seeing the questioning look in Salvatore's eyes.

'Why do you have to be back then?'

'Personal reasons.'

Darcey briefly considered explaining why she had to return to London at the end of the summer, but she was reluctant to reveal that she was a member of the famous Hart family. She'd had previous experiences of people trying to befriend her because of her family connections—not least her ex-husband.

Memories crowded her mind: an image of Marcus in *their* bed with a naked woman. He hadn't even had the decency to look repentant, she remembered. But worse humiliation had followed in the ensuing row, when he had admitted that he had not married her because he loved her, but for the kudos of being Joshua Hart's son-in-law and the potential boost that would give his own acting career.

In the eighteen months since her divorce the pain of Marcus's betrayal had faded, but deep down Darcey felt ashamed that she had been such a gullible fool as to trust him. It was not a mistake she intended to make again.

There was no reason for her to give Salvatore details of her private life, she assured herself. She had agreed to go to Sicily in her professional capacity and the only thing he needed to know was that she was prepared to carry out her job to the best of her ability.

'Because of the fire at the winery I have decided to return to Sicily tomorrow,' he told her. 'Can you be ready to leave mid-morning? We'll travel on my private jet. Give me your address and I'll send the car for you.'

The man was a steamroller, Darcey thought ruefully. She shook her head. 'I have a few things to do. I won't be ready to leave with you. I'll book a commercial flight and come at the weekend.'

Salvatore was used to his staff following orders without question, and he felt a flare of irritation that Darcey seemed determined to argue about everything. 'It would suit me better if you come tomorrow.'

It occurred to him that if she had accepted the salary he had offered he would have had more control over her. He still could not quite get over the fact that she had ripped up the cheque, and he was aware that now the balance of power was in her favour. For the first time in his life money had not been the solution to a problem.

'But it will suit *me* better to fly out at the weekend,' Darcey said coolly, refusing to drop her gaze from his hard stare. 'I'm having lunch with my parents tomorrow.'

'Fine. I'll delay our flight time for a few hours and we will leave in the afternoon. You were going to go to France on Friday,' Salvatore reminded her. 'What difference will it make if you leave with me two days earlier? Rosa will be happier if you fly out with us—especially now that Sharon has gone.'

Darcey sighed. She suspected that Salvatore understood she had formed an emotional attachment to his deaf daughter and would not want to disappoint the little girl. 'I'll be ready to leave at three o'clock,' she said resignedly. She stood up from the table. 'But now you will have to excuse me so that I can go home and finish packing.'

'I'll escort you to your car.'

He walked across the room and held open the door. Darcey's stomach muscles clenched as their bodies brushed when she passed him. She breathed in the sensual musk of his cologne and wondered why he used it when the black stubble shading his jaw indicated that he had not shaved today. With his dark, brooding good looks he reminded her of a pirate, and she sensed that he was just as dangerous.

In the hall she slipped on her jacket, thankful that it concealed her treacherous body. Her breasts felt heavy, and she would be mortified if he noticed that her nipples had hardened and were straining against the thin material of her blouse. She followed him out of the house. The night air cooled her hot face, but her fierce awareness of him did not lessen as she walked beside him along the pavement to where her car was parked. She must have been mad to have agreed to go to Sicily with him, she thought despairingly. *It's not too late to pull out*, a voice in her head whispered. She hadn't signed a contract. She unlocked the Mini and slid into the driver's seat. Her fingers fumbled to insert the key in the ignition.

'Rosa will be excited when I tell her that you will be staying at the castle with us.' Salvatore held the car door open and leaned down so that his face was almost level with hers.

Oh, hell! Her gaze was drawn involuntarily to his stern mouth before lifting to his eyes. Something flickered in his dark expression and for a breathless few seconds she thought he was going to lower his head and kiss her. Time slowed and her heartbeat raced. His warm breath whispered across her mouth and she moistened her lips with the tip of her tongue in an unconscious invitation.

'Goodnight, Darcey.' Abruptly he stepped back and closed the car door.

Darcey tried to quash her disappointment. Of *course* she had not wanted him to kiss her, she assured herself as she turned the key in the ignition. She would go to Sicily for Rosa's sake, but she intended that her relationship with Salvatore would remain firmly within the boundaries of employer and employee.

'Hello, darling! What are you doing here?'

Joshua Hart greeted Darcey with a vague smile when she arrived at her parents' house in London's Notting Hill the following day. Her father held open the front door to allow her to step into the hallway.

'I thought you were on holiday.'

'I told you the last time I saw you that I going away at the beginning of July.' Darcey forbore to ask her father why he was wearing pyjamas and a dressing gown at midday. 'I've come to have lunch with you and Mum.'

'Oh, well—your mother never said. No one tells me anything,' Joshua grumbled. He pushed open his study door. 'You won't mind if I don't join you? I'm up to my eyes in *Othello*. The new production opens at the National Theatre next week and I'll never be ready,' he stated dramatically. He paused in the doorway and turned his piercing blue eyes on Darcey. 'Have you been studying the script I sent you? Remember, rehearsals for my play begin at the end of September.'

'I haven't forgotten,' Darcey said drily. She carried on down the hall and found her mother in the kitchen.

'I'm sorry about your father,' Claudia murmured ruefully. 'I reminded him three times that you were coming for lunch, but you know how forgetful he is when he's involved with work. He has locked himself away in his study for days while he studies this next role.'

Darcey understood that Joshua's artistic temperament and his perfectionism could make him selfish, but she could not help feeling hurt that he was too busy to have lunch with her. The sense of rejection she had some-times felt as a child returned to haunt her and gave her added insight into how Rosa must feel when Salvatore ignored her. The little girl was desperate for more atten-tion from her father.

'I expect you're looking forward to your trip to France?' Claudia said.

'Actually, there's been a change of plan. I'm going to Sicily to give speech therapy to a deaf child who has re-cently had cochlear implants fitted.' Darcey handed her mother the Maidenhair Fern that she had brought with her. 'Will you take care of my plant while I'm away? It needs a lot of TLC.'

Her mother sighed. 'Oh, darling, you need a break. You've been working so hard lately, and you've had so much to cope with, what with Marcus and the divorce. And I know you have been concerned about my illness. My consultant has given me the all-clear, by the way. So you can stop worrying about me. I really think you should reconsider taking this job. Isn't there someone else who can work with this child?'

'Rosa is a sweet little girl who has been deaf since she was a baby and is unable to talk,' Darcey explained. 'I'm optimistic that speech and language therapy will make a huge difference to her life.'

'I know you will do your best for her,' Claudia said softly, aware that once Darcey had made up her mind she would not be detracted. 'But I hope you'll have a bit of relaxation time. What are Rosa's parents like?'

'Her mother died when she was a baby.' Darcey hesi-tated. 'Her father is…' she searched for a word to describe Salvatore '…formidable.'

Her mother gave her a searching look. 'He sounds in-triguing. Is he good-looking?'

'What does that have to do with anything?' She met Claudia's amused gaze and shrugged helplessly. 'I guess he is, in a dangerous sort of way.'

'Now you're worrying me, darling. The man is formidable, dangerous, and you're attracted to him,' Claudia added perceptively.

Darcey knew there was no point in denying it. Sometimes she thought her mother possessed psychic powers. 'Salvatore Castellano is handsome, admittedly, but he's also arrogant, egotistical—oh, and he likes to have his own way.'

Claudia laughed. 'Well, that's a trait you both share. It sounds as though sparks might fly in Sicily.'

Darcey shook her head. 'There's no need for you to worry. I don't intend anything to happen between us.'

'What a pity. A sizzling affair with a sexy Sicilian would do you the world of good!'

'*Mum!*'

'It's about time you put your marriage behind you,' Claudia said unrepentantly. 'You've never explained what really happened between you and Marcus, or the reason why you broke up—although I have my suspicions that he hurt you badly. But he's history now. You need to move on and allow romance back into your life.'

Darcey looked away from her mother. She had never spoken about what Marcus had done—how he had made a fool of her and tricked her into marriage by pretending to love her when in fact he had seen her as means of furthering his acting career because of her famous theatrical family. It was so humiliating that she had vowed never to reveal the truth to anyone.

As for her having an affair with Salvatore—the idea was laughable. 'Romance is definitely *not* on the cards with Salvatore Castellano,' she insisted.

Last night she had been unable to sleep for thinking about him, and had decided that she must have imagined that he'd seemed about to kiss her. He was not attracted to her, and the sooner she got over her ridiculous fascination with him the better.

'I'll be going to Sicily on a strictly professional basis,' she told her mother. 'I've agreed to stay for three months, so you can tell Dad I'll be back in London for rehearsals at the end of September, as I promised.'

'Your father is so pleased that you've agreed to perform in his new play.' Claudia gave her daughter an understanding smile. 'I know he put you under a lot of pressure to take the role, but he thinks you are perfect for it. Joshua has always believed that you could have had a wonderful career as an actress.'

Darcey sighed, feeling the familiar pang of guilt that she had disappointed her father by being the only member of the Hart family not to have become a professional actor. She loved the career she had chosen, and had no regrets that she had not gone to drama school like her brother and sisters, but there was still a need inside her to appease her father and earn his approval.

Joshua had written his latest play expecting that his wife would take the lead role, but Claudia had decided to take a break from acting while she recuperated after treatment for skin cancer.

'You are the only person apart from your mother who I can envisage playing the role of Edith,' Joshua had told Darcey when she had argued that either Mina or her older sister Victoria would be better for the part. 'You proved when you used to perform with Speak Out that you are a talented actress. If you won't play Edith then I'll abandon the project until such time—God willing—that Claudia is well enough to return to the stage.'

It had been blatant emotional blackmail by her father, Darcey thought wryly. But she had agreed to perform in the play. Partly because she hoped it would give her an opportunity to form a closer relationship with Joshua, but also out of curiosity, to find out if she *did* possess the same ability to act as the other members of her family. Shyer than her brother and sisters, all her life she had compared herself to her confident and extrovert relatives. Now she had the chance to prove to herself and to her father that she was a true Hart.

It was early evening when Salvatore's private jet landed at Catania Airport and they transferred to the car that was waiting to collect them. Rosa's child seat took up more than one passenger space, and Darcey was squashed up close to Salvatore. She could feel his hard thigh muscles through her lightweight skirt.

She turned her head and stared out of the window at the spectacular Sicilian countryside. The sun was low in the sky and cast a mellow light over the checkerboard of green and gold fields dotted with patches of vibrant red flowers. In the distance Mount Etna towered over the land, its upper slopes dusted with snow even in the summer. Darcey knew that Etna was the biggest active volcano in Europe. A stream of white vapour spouted from its summit, but to her relief the fiery giant was not spewing scorching lava today.

Unfortunately admiring the beauty of her surroundings did not lessen her fierce awareness of the man beside her. Her resolve to ignore her attraction to Salvatore had been blown sky-high when he had turned up at her tiny terraced house at precisely three o'clock. She had opened the door expecting to find his driver had come to collect her, but instead it had been Salvatore on the doorstep, dressed in a superbly tailored pale grey suit that made him look more like a business tycoon than the leather jacket had the previous day, but no less sexy.

She had felt strangely reluctant to invite him into her home, but she'd had no choice but to ask for his help in lifting her huge suitcase. Packing twelve pairs of shoes had probably been excessive, she conceded.

He had seemed like a giant in her small house, but it was not just his height and athletic build that made him impossible to ignore. He possessed a powerful magnetism that was accentuated by his brooding good looks. When they had walked through the airport she had noticed the attention he had received from other women—although to be fair he had seemed unconcerned by the excitement he generated.

She must have been mad to come to Sicily with him when he unsettled her so much.

Darcey unconsciously lifted her hand to the pendant around her neck and traced its familiar shape, as she often did when she was troubled.

'Your necklace is interesting. The stones are the exact shade of green as your eyes.'

Her eyes flew to Salvatore's face. 'It's a four-leaf clover, which in Irish folklore is a symbol of good luck. My father gave it to me on my wedding day.'

His brows lifted. 'But it didn't work? The pendant did not bring you good luck in your marriage as you are now divorced.'

'It would have taken more than a lucky charm for my marriage to Marcus to have worked.'

Salvatore heard the faint tremor in her voice and was curious, despite his resolve to keep his relationship with her on a strictly professional footing. He did not know what had come over him last night when he had been tempted to kiss her. And now he could not dismiss the image in his mind of the peridot pendant resting between her naked breasts.

Desire tugged in his groin, and for once he struggled to bring his body under control. He had ended his affair with his last mistress months ago—no doubt he was suffering from sexual frustration, he thought self-derisively. He had spent the flight to Sicily working through a backlog of paperwork, but his attempts to ignore Darcey had failed and he had read one financial report three times before it made sense.

Last night he had been unable to sleep. His thoughts had centred on his old friend Pietro, but for some reason Darcey had also crept into his mind. Today his temper was not improved by the fact that she had clearly enjoyed a restful night and looked perkily pretty in a pastel pink skirt and a white blouse sprigged with pink daisies. Her copper-brown bob of hair swung around her face, and every time she turned her head he inhaled the lemony scent of her shampoo.

For a moment he questioned whether it had been a good idea to bring her to Sicily. It was too late to change his mind now, he thought grimly. He was impressed by her kindness to Rosa and felt sure she was the best person to teach her to speak. His daughter was all that mattered, Salvatore reminded himself. For a number of reasons he was determined to ignore his inconvenient attraction to Darcey.

It was hot in the car and he opened the window, hoping that the fresh air rushing in would help to ease his headache. He closed his eyes and snatches of memory flashed into his mind.

He was travelling fast in a car and could feel the wind on his face. It was a sports car, and the sunroof was open.

The night-time sky surrounded him. The trees at the side of the road flashed past in a blur. He could see the needle on the speedometer rise higher and higher but he could not brake. He could see the bend in the road ahead but he couldn't turn the steering wheel…

Santa Madre! Salvatore's eyes flew open. He could feel beads of sweat on his brow and his hand shook as he raked his hand through his hair. *What the hell had that been about?* For the first time in four years he had remembered something about the accident, but his mind had played tricks on him. He *knew* he had been driving the car on the night of the accident, so why had he just had a memory of sitting in the passenger seat? It did not make sense. Perhaps the past would forever be hidden from him, he thought bitterly. It was his punishment for causing his wife's death.

He turned his head and found Darcey looking at him oddly. 'Are you all right? You had your eyes closed and you groaned as if you were in pain.'

'I'm fine,' he said curtly. 'I suffer from migraines occasionally,' he growled, when Darcey continued to stare at him.

He did not want her concern, or the sympathy that flared in her green eyes. The breeze from the open window carried the delicate floral scent of her perfume to him and he felt a sudden longing to press his lips to her slender white throat.

Muttering a savage oath beneath his breath, he jerked his eyes from her, and to his relief the car came to a halt in front of the ornate metal gates at the entrance to the Castellano Estate.

CHAPTER FOUR

Two SECURITY GUARDS were on duty and immediately activated the gates so that they swung open. The car drove along a gravel driveway which then split into three roads. One led to a large white house that Salvatore told Darcey was where his father lived. His brother, Sergio, lived with his wife and son in a villa on another part of the estate.

Above the pine trees Darcey saw tall stone turrets, and a few minutes later she caught her breath when the car rounded a bend and an imposing castle came into view.

The brickwork was ancient and crumbling in places. Over centuries the stones had faded and were now a mellow sandy colour that deepened to gold in the late sunshine. The arched windows were flanked by thick wooden shutters and the huge front door looked as though it had been hewn from solid oak and had once repelled warring invaders.

'Wow!' she murmured as she climbed out of the car.

Salvatore smiled at her reaction. It was the first time Darcey had seen him smile properly and her heart lurched when his stern features softened. She did not know what had happened in the car, when he had seemed so tense, but as he looked up at the castle he visibly relaxed.

'Welcome to Torre de'Aquila. A castle was first built here in the thirteenth century, and gained its name because of the eagles that nested in the highest tower. Parts of the original building still remain, and eagles still nest in the tower. Look…'

He pointed to the sky and Darcey looked up and spotted a bird of prey with a distinctive hooked beak and huge wingspan circling the tower.

'It's a Bonelli's Eagle—sometimes called a white eagle because of the white feathers on its underside.'

'I've never seen an eagle in the wild before.'

Darcey felt awed as she watched the bird glide gracefully across the sky. The majestic eagle seemed utterly suited to the ancient castle. She glanced at the imposing man beside her. With hard features that could have been chiselled from stone, and his long dark hair, Salvatore looked as though he belonged to this rugged fortress. The first time she had seen him she had thought of him as a warrior knight: proud, noble and dangerous.

He was a serious threat to her peace of mind, Darcey acknowledged ruefully. It was safer to concentrate on Rosa, and she smiled at the little girl as Salvatore lifted her out of the car.

Can we go swimming, Papa? Rosa signed.

Salvatore shook his head. *Not now. Perhaps I'll have time to take you tomorrow.*

'It's important that you use language at the same time that you are signing to Rosa,' Darcey told him. 'Now that she can hear with the implants I think she will soon start to understand speech.'

She noticed the disappointment on the little girl's face and recalled how Rosa had told her that swimming was her favourite activity. 'Couldn't you take her for a swim?' She pleaded Rosa's case. 'It would do her good after she's spent the past few hours sitting in a plane or a car.'

Salvatore shook his head. He always visited Pietro as

soon as he returned to the Castellano Estate, but today, instead of going to Pietro's cottage, he would be going to the mortuary.

'There is something important I have to do,' he told Darcey brusquely.

'To do with work, I suppose?' Her voice was sharp and accusatory.

Salvatore's jaw clenched. He felt bad enough about disappointing Rosa, and Darcey's words added to his guilt. But he knew he would not be good company right now when all he could think about was the kindly man who had been a surrogate father to him.

'Your job is to give Rosa speech therapy, not to lecture me on my parenting methods,' he reminded her coldly.

Darcey stared at his arrogant face and wondered if she'd imagined that he had actually smiled a few minutes earlier. He looked away from her, towards the castle, and growled something in Italian as the front door swung open and a woman appeared.

'I wasn't expecting Lydia to be here,' he muttered.

For a moment Darcey wondered if the platinum blonde, heavily made-up woman was his mistress—or perhaps an ex-mistress, as Salvatore did not sound overly pleased to see her. She darted him a questioning glance.

'Lydia is my mother-in-law. She comes fairly often to see Rosa. Curiously, her visits usually coincide with her needing money,' he added in a bone-dry tone.

Rosa slipped her small hand into Darcey's as they walked up the stone steps leading to the castle's entrance, where her grandmother was waiting. The older woman gave Darcey a curious glance before turning her attention to her granddaughter.

'Hello, sweetie,' Lydia did not sign, but spoke to Rosa in a loud voice. She frowned when the little girl made no response and looked at Salvatore. 'I thought you said Rosa was going to have an operation that would make her speak?'

'She has had a procedure in which cochlear implants were fitted, allowing her to hear sounds,' he explained. 'It will take time for her to learn to talk. Ms Rivers is a speech therapist who is going to help her.'

He made formal introductions. Lydia seemed friendly enough, but Darcey was conscious of the older woman's pale blue eyes flicking between her and Salvatore as they all walked into the castle.

Stepping through the front door, Darcey stopped dead and looked around in amazement. 'What a beautiful place!'

The entrance hall was a huge, airy space, filled with light that streamed through the arched windows onto the flagstone floor. Darcey had imagined the castle to be a gloomy place, but the panelling on the walls was a warm cherrywood, and the rooms she could see leading off the hall were painted white and were bright and welcoming. Colourful tapestries hung on many of the walls, and the antique furniture had been highly polished—and a faint scent of beeswax hung in the air.

Her eyes were drawn to the picture on the wall directly facing the front door. It was a photograph enlarged to life-size of a strikingly attractive brunette who looked as though she had been poured into her scarlet silk dress. The picture was impossible to miss or ignore.

Following Darcey's gaze, Lydia said, 'That's my daughter—Adriana. She was a top model and worked with all the famous designers. Shortly before she died she had been offered a role in a film. It was a tragedy that she was taken so young, before she had a chance to fulfil her potential—wasn't it, Salvatore?'

He made no response, and his hard features were unfathomable, but for a second Darcey glimpsed a haunted expression in his eyes that startled her. She sensed an undercurrent of tension between him and Lydia, and the atmosphere in the hall suddenly made her skin prickle, as if Adriana's ghost had walked past.

In a desperate attempt to break the edgy silence, she said to Salvatore, 'You have a beautiful home. I expect your wife loved living in a castle?'

'Why do we have to live in this crumbling pile of bricks? I want to move to a city. I'll die of boredom here...'

Salvatore frowned as the voice in his head faded away. It had been a voice from his past and he knew with certainty that he had heard his wife. 'No...' he said slowly. 'Adriana hated it here.'

Lydia gave a loud laugh that sounded curiously strained to Darcey. 'Of course she didn't hate the castle. The two of you were so happy here, Salvatore.'

'So you keep reminding me,' he said obliquely. He glanced at Darcey. 'One of the staff will show you to your room and bring your luggage up. This is Armond.' He indicated the portly man dressed in a butler's uniform who had just joined them. 'He will attend to you. Perhaps you would be kind enough to stay with Rosa? I have yet to arrange to hire another nanny, and right now there are other matters I must deal with. Excuse me.'

He strode out of the castle, but as he walked down the front steps Darcey noticed that he was limping, as if his injured leg was painful. She sighed. He was such an enigmatic man. She sensed that the air of mystery surrounding him was linked to his dead wife.

She gave a start when Lydia's voice broke into her thoughts. 'You must forgive my son-in-law if he appears abrupt,' the older woman murmured. 'He was so in love with my daughter and has never got over her death.' She gave Darcey a calculating look. 'Occasionally he has affairs with women, but they mean nothing to him. I'm afraid no other woman will ever take Adriana's place in Salvatore's heart.'

Darcey was reading Rosa a bedtime story when Salvatore walked into the room. The little girl had forgotten about swimming in her excitement at showing Darcey her bedroom, which was next door to the nursery, and when she saw her father her face lit up. To Darcey's surprise he came and sat on the edge of the bed. His hair was tangled and he smelled of smoke. Rosa gave him a puzzled look.

Why have you got black on your face, Papa? she asked in sign language.

He rubbed a hand over his cheek and looked rueful when he saw smears of soot on his fingers. *There has been a fire at the winery. I went to see the damage,* he signed. He dropped a kiss on Rosa's brow. *Goodnight, angel.*

Salvatore stood up, but as he went to turn off the lamp Darcey stopped him. 'Leave the light on. Rosa doesn't like the dark.'

'How do you know that?' he demanded as he followed her out of the room.

'She told me.' Darcey bit back a comment that if he'd paid his daughter more attention he would have known about her fear of the dark.

'I understand from Armond that you did not have dinner with Rosa?' he said.

'I wasn't hungry.' Noticing lines of strain around his

face, she said quietly, 'I'm sorry about the fire. Is there much damage?'

Salvatore pictured Pietro's lifeless body and grief roughened his voice. 'The winery can be rebuilt, but the men who were burned in the fire will take much longer to recover.'

'You look tired,' she said softly. 'Have you eaten tonight?'

Her gentle concern was something Salvatore had never experienced before, and he could not cope with it tonight when his emotions were raw.

'You sound like a wife,' he mocked. 'I can look after myself.'

Darcey flushed. 'That's good, because any woman foolish enough to marry you would need the patience of a saint.' She swung away from him, feeling guilty that she had snapped at him, because after all his wife was dead.

'Darcey…' He caught hold of her arm and turned her back to face him. 'I'm sorry. That was crass of me.' He exhaled heavily. 'Seeing the burned winery was… upsetting.'

It was the first time in his life that Salvatore had ever revealed his feelings to another person and his shock was mirrored in Darcey's eyes. What was it about this woman that got to him and made him act out of character? he asked himself. He hated the idea that he was in any way vulnerable, but Pietro's death, and the startling flashbacks to his past, were making him feel as though a layer of his flesh had been peeled away.

He glanced ruefully at his smoke-blackened clothes. 'Give me five minutes to shower and then we'll have dinner on the terrace. Lydia won't be eating with us tonight, and we can spend some time getting to know each other.'

Darcey found the prospect frankly terrifying—especially when his harsh features softened and he gave her a sexy smile that turned her insides to marshmallow.

'Is that really necessary?' she said coolly. 'I'm merely an employee, and I'm sure you don't take a personal interest in the other members of your staff.'

'As a matter of fact all the staff at the castle have worked here for years and I know them very well. You are going to be living at Torre d'Aquila for the next three months, Darcey,' he reminded her. 'I would like you to feel comfortable in my home and with me.'

Comfortable was not the way she would describe the way she felt when she stepped out of the French doors fifteen minutes later, Darcey thought derisively. Salvatore walked across the terrace towards her and she felt her stomach swoop as she took in his appearance. Wearing tailored black trousers and a loose-fitting white shirt unbuttoned at the throat, he had an air of brooding sensuality that set her pulse racing.

She had resisted the temptation to change her skirt and blouse for a more seductive outfit, and had simply brushed her hair and added a slick of pink gloss to her lips. It was not as if she wanted him to find her attractive, she reminded herself. But her heart thudded when he halted in front of her and his dark eyes rested on her face. She caught her breath when he lifted his hand and tucked her hair behind her ear.

'You are very lovely, Darcey,' he murmured, half to himself. His gaze lingered on her mouth and the atmosphere on the terrace altered subtly, became heavy with unspoken sexual awareness.

'We can go inside if you are cold?' He broke the spell and stepped away from her.

Darcey wondered if he'd guessed that it was not the

air temperature that had made her shiver. 'I'm fine—just tired from travelling today,' she lied.

He held out a chair at the table. 'Then let's eat.'

Armond served a simple supper of seafood risotto accompanied by a crisp white wine from the Castellano estate. Darcey felt herself relax as she sipped her wine, although perversely her awareness of Salvatore intensified.

'Tell me about Darcey Rivers,' he invited, his eyes meeting hers across the table.

'What do you want to know?' She ran through a mental list of subjects that were off-limits. Her famous family she preferred not to talk about, and her marriage and her ex-husband's behaviour would never be open for discussion.

'Why did you choose speech therapy as a career?'

Work was a safe topic. 'I think I told you that my sister is deaf? Growing up with Mina gave me an understanding of how important communication is. Mina had learned to speak before she lost her hearing, but for Rosa speech is a new concept. It will take time and patience for her to learn language skills.' She hesitated. 'I can give Rosa speech therapy sessions every day, but they won't magically enable her to speak. Therapy has to be continual, and it has to become part of your life as much as Rosa's. I will need to work with you as much as with her, and teach you how you can help her. It is important that you make time for your daughter. I don't mean ten minutes at bedtime when you say goodnight to her. I'm talking about a serious commitment to spend several hours every day giving her your undivided attention. That means coming out of your office and switching off your mobile phone so that you can play games and read stories to her. Surely that's not too much to ask?' she said huskily when he made no response.

He looked away from her, but not before she had glimpsed a flicker of pain in his eyes.

'Rosa always preferred to do those sorts of things with her nanny, Luisa,' Salvatore said roughly. 'And although she had not formed the same close bond with Sharon she seemed happier in her company than mine.'

It was on the tip of Darcey's tongue to tell him that if he wasn't so remote with his daughter she would probably feel more confident with him.

'I'm sure Rosa would love to play with you.' She hesitated, aware of a need to be diplomatic. 'I think she might respond better if you could relax a bit more when you are with her. She's your daughter, after all. Perhaps it would help if you could think back to when you were a child and the games you used to play with your parents?'

'My mother walked out when I was five, and when I was seven my father sent me to boarding school in England. I don't remember spending time with either of my parents, and they certainly did not play games with me.'

Shaken by the harshness of his tone, Darcey did not know what to say. It was not surprising that Salvatore found it hard to connect with his daughter when it sounded as though his own childhood had been so loveless, she mused. He must have been traumatised from being abandoned by his mother when he had been so young. She thought of her close-knit family and felt a stirring of sympathy for the stern-faced man seated opposite her.

'Why did your father send you away to school?'

'He said he thought it would be better for me to grow up with companions of my own age.' Salvatore shrugged. 'But I believe the reality was that he wasn't interested in me. He was devastated when my mother left and focused entirely on work and furthering the success of the Castellano Group.'

'And now history is repeating itself,' Darcey said quietly. 'Rosa has no mother, and her father spends too much time working rather than giving her the attention she needs.'

Darcey's criticism was not unfounded, Salvatore acknowledged grimly. He did not know how to be a father to his daughter. The truth buried deep in his heart was that he was afraid to get too close to her. What if he actually couldn't be a good father? What if he failed Rosa as his parents had failed him? Since she was a baby he had found it easier to hand her over to the care of a professional nanny.

'I do not require your opinion on how I choose to bring up my daughter,' he said curtly. 'All I'm interested in is your expertise as a speech therapist.'

Who was he kidding? Salvatore thought derisively. He could not ignore his attraction to Darcey when every time he looked at her he felt a primitive urge to pull her into his arms and claim her lips with his. With her shiny bob of hair and her buttoned-to-the-neck blouse she looked as wholesome as Mary Poppins, but her lush mouth held a promise of sensuality that he knew he must resist.

Dio, he had no right to want to make love to her when he could not even remember the woman he had been married to. His mother-in-law constantly told him that he had loved Adriana, and because of his amnesia he had no alternative but to believe Lydia. But when he looked at photographs of his wife he felt nothing.

He looked up as the butler hurried across the terrace.

'*Signor*, one of the maids heard Miss Rosa crying. When she checked she found the child distraught.'

Salvatore immediately got up from the table. 'Thank

you, Armond. I'll go up to her.' He looked at Darcey. 'It might be better if you come too. Rosa sometimes has nightmares and she might prefer you to comfort her.'

The soul-wrenching sounds of a child's sobs were audible as Darcey hurried after Salvatore up the staircase, and when she followed him into the nursery the sight of Rosa's tear-stained face made her heart ache. With the cochlear implant device switched off Rosa could not hear, and she was obviously too upset to communicate in sign language. The terrified expression on her face indicated that she had not fully woken from a nightmare.

Salvatore hurried over to the bed, but instead of lifting the little girl into his arms he hesitantly patted her hair and glanced at Darcey. 'She feels hot. Do you think she's ill?'

Rosa's cries had quietened to soft whimpers that tore on his heart. He wanted to hold her in his arms and comfort her, but the fearful expression in her eyes stopped him. What had she dreamed of that had upset her so badly? Rosa's nightmares were becoming more frequent, and Salvatore wondered if the trauma of losing her mother when she had been a baby was somehow the cause. Gripped by guilt, he stepped back from the bed so that Darcey could comfort Rosa.

Darcey felt the little girl's brow. 'She's not feverish. It's likely that she got too warm under the covers—that could have triggered a nightmare.'

She sat on the bed and signed to Rosa—*It's all right. You're safe. You just had a bad dream. Would you like me to stay with you for a while?*

Rosa nodded and flung her arms around Darcey's neck, clinging to her as if she never wanted to let go. Darcey stroked her hair and gradually the child grew calmer.

Salvatore watched them, envious of Darcey's easy rapport with Rosa, and once again he was struck by her inherent kindness. His phone rang. He swore beneath his breath and made to cut the call—until he saw that Sergio was on the line.

'It's my brother,' he told Darcey. 'He said he would update me on the condition of the men injured in the fire. Would you mind staying with Rosa for a while?'

She nodded. 'I'll sit with her until she falls back to sleep. At least my room is only next door if she stirs in the night.'

Promise you'll stay with me in case the monsters come back, Rosa signed.

Darcey gave her a reassuring smile. *I promise,* she signed back.

She was touched by the little girl's obvious loneliness and her eagerness for them to be friends. She watched Rosa's eyelashes drift down but decided to stay for another half-hour to make sure the child was deeply asleep. It was warm in the bedroom, and she undid the top few buttons of her blouse before lying back on the bedspread. Rosa immediately snuggled closer and Darcey's mothering instincts kicked in. She put her arm around the sleeping child.

When Salvatore walked back into the nursery half an hour later he was greeted by the soft sigh of breathing from the woman and child fast asleep on the bed. Rosa was tucked up between the sheets and Darcey was curled on the bedspread beside her.

As he crossed the room Darcey rolled onto her back and he saw that her blouse was partly open, revealing a tantalising glimpse of the upper swell of her breasts above a sexy semi-sheer bra. His body responded instantly and his erection strained beneath his trousers. Once again he asked himself why he had brought her to Sicily and he seriously considered sending her back to England. She was a complication he could do without, he thought grimly.

He moved closer to the bed and saw that even in her sleep Rosa was clutching hold of Darcey's hand. He could not put his daughter through the trauma of separating her from someone else she had bonded with. It had been hard enough for her when first Luisa had left, and then Sharon. Rosa needed a mother figure to take the place of the mother he had deprived her of. He was not expecting Darcey to take on that role, of course, but Rosa needed help from an expert speech therapist.

It was warm in the bedroom, and Rosa's face was flushed from where she was lying close to Darcey. Concerned that if the little girl became too hot she might have another nightmare, Salvatore touched Darcey's shoulder, intending to wake her. He hesitated, remembering that she had said she was tired from travelling. Her bedroom adjoined to the nursery, and it seemed more sensible to carry her through to her room.

Neither of the sleepers stirred when he lifted Darcey into his arms. Her neat bob of burnished-copper hair framed her face and her long eyelashes made golden crescents on her creamy cheeks. She weighed next to nothing. It should be the easiest thing to carry her into the other room, deposit her on the bed and leave. But the delicate fragrance of her perfume assailed his senses.

Jaw tense, he strode through the connecting door. As he leaned down and placed her on the bed she murmured a soft protest and looped her arm around his neck, pulling his head down so that his face was centimetres from hers.

Madonna, this was not what he had intended to happen. His conscience insisted that he must wake her up, but his body was remembering how he had wanted to kiss her on the terrace. He had been transfixed by her soft pink mouth and desire had swept like wildfire through his veins.

He must fight his fierce attraction to Darcey, Salvatore told himself. His instincts warned him that she was not like the sophisticated women he'd had affairs with in the past. She was curiously innocent, and he wondered if she'd had any lovers since her marriage had ended.

His eyes were drawn to the creamy mounds of her breasts and the darker skin of her nipples, which he could see through her semi-transparent bra. This was madness! Every muscle in his body clenched as he resisted slanting his mouth over her moist lips that had parted slightly, as if she wanted him to kiss her. Could she really be unaware of what she was doing?

Carefully he tried to ease away from her, but she curled her arm tighter around his neck and gave a little mew of protest. 'Please…' she whispered, and Salvatore's self-control shattered.

CHAPTER FIVE

DARCEY'S DREAM WAS becoming increasingly erotic. It had begun with the shadowy figure of a man—a strong, powerful man—who held her in his muscular arms. She felt safe with the man, even though she did not know him. His face was hidden from her but he seemed familiar, and his musky, masculine scent was intoxicating, arousing an ache inside her that she had not felt for a long time.

His broad chest felt warm and solid beneath her fingertips—surprisingly solid, considering that he was only a dream. She was aware of his hands on her body and she felt his breath whisper across her lips. Why didn't he kiss her? She wanted him to—just as she wanted him to move his hands over her, up to her breasts and down to the junction between her thighs. She moved restlessly and lifted her hips in a silent plea for him to touch her there…

'Please…' she whispered. She wished she could see his face, but it did not matter, because now his mouth was on hers, as light as gossamer, teasing her lips apart.

No man had ever kissed her so beautifully.

The thought pushed through the fog clouding Darcey's brain and she became aware that she was lying on a bed. She gave a puzzled frown. She had only ever been to bed with one man, so the dream man must be…

'Marcus?'

'Who the hell is Marcus?' a harsh voice demanded.

Darcey's eyes flew open and shock ripped through her as she stared at Salvatore's darkly handsome face. *He* had been the man in her dream?

'What are you doing?' Heat flooded her cheeks when she glanced down and saw that her blouse was gaping open. She remembered that she had felt hot and unfastened a few of the buttons when she had lain on the bed with Rosa. Now she was in her own room, lying on her bed, and Salvatore was leaning over her, his chiselled face all angles and planes in the moonlight.

He must have carried her in here, but why? Her eyes widened as she remembered the feel of firm lips on hers. She hadn't been dreaming. Salvatore had kissed her, and if her memory served her right she had kissed him back.

'How dare you take advantage of me.'

He frowned. 'I did not take advantage of you.'

Despite his denial, Salvatore's conscience prickled uncomfortably. He knew he should have woken her, or left her sleeping and walked out of her room, but when she had said *please* in that sexy, whispery voice he had decided that she must be awake.

'You were aware of what you were doing—and that it was me you were with,' he growled.

'I was asleep and dreaming.'

'If so, then you were dreaming of me. You begged me to kiss you.'

Thank God she hadn't voiced the other things she had wanted him to do to her, Darcey thought, feeling sick with embarrassment as she remembered how she had longed for him to slide his hand between her legs, where he would have discovered the moist heat of her arousal. She had been asleep, she tried to assure herself. But innate honesty forced her to acknowledge that she had recognised the man in her dream.

She had been thinking about Salvatore while she had waited for Rosa to fall asleep and must have dozed off with his image still in her subconscious. It was also true that she had asked him to kiss her. She shuddered with mortification at the memory. But he must have realised that she had not been fully aware of her actions, she thought angrily.

'There's no getting away from the fact that you behaved dishonourably.'

Salvatore's hot Sicilian pride flared. Attacking his honour was going too far.

'You can try to kid yourself all you like, but this isn't going to go away for either of us.' He leaned over her, placing his hands flat on the bed on either side of her head so that he could stare into her wide green eyes. 'Your eyes give away your secrets, *cara*. They tell me you are interested in me.'

'I certainly am not,' she denied, too quickly.

The corners of his mouth curled in a sardonic half-smile. 'Liar. You felt it just as I did—the second I walked into your office.'

Darcey was trapped by his mesmerising gaze. 'Felt what?' she whispered.

'Sexual attraction, chemistry—call it what you like. The point is that within the first twenty seconds of us meeting we were both imagining making love on your desk.'

She gasped. 'I did no such thing.' She was outraged by his boldness, and mortified that he had seen what she had so desperately tried to hide. The truth was she had never felt such fierce physical awareness of a man. Not even Marcus, with his model-perfect looks, had evoked the fierce surge of lust that Salvatore Castellano incited in her.

'Tell me you don't want me to kiss you and I'll walk out of the door before you can blink,' he taunted.

Obviously she was going to tell the arrogant so and so to get lost, Darcey thought furiously. It was just that the words seemed to be stuck in her throat. Her gaze was trapped by the predatory glint in Salvatore's eyes. She caught her lower lip between her teeth and his eyes narrowed.

The sexual tension simmering between them was unbearable. Something had to give. Her heart lurched when he lowered his head towards her.

'You want this as much as I do,' Salvatore growled.

She had got under his skin since the moment he had walked into her office and she had blown his preconceptions of the mature speech therapist he had expected to meet sky-high. Ordinarily he would have dismissed his reaction to her as an inconvenience. But the news of Pietro's death had ripped his insides out. He had been genuinely fond of his old friend. The elderly vintner had been more of a father to him than Tito, and he knew that Pietro had loved him like a son.

It hurt him to think of Pietro. He wanted to block out thoughts of death with a reaffirmation of life and lose himself in the sensual promise of Darcey's soft mouth and slender body. And she would not deny him. Her pupils were dilated and her breasts rose and fell jerkily, drawing his attention to the hard points of her nipples that he could see clearly beneath her sheer bra.

Darcey lifted her hand to push Salvatore away. At least that was what she intended to do. But when she touched his shoulder and felt his powerful bunched muscles her common sense disappeared and feminine instinct took over, so that she spread her fingers wide and felt the warmth of his body through his shirt. She could not tell him she did not want him to kiss her because it would be a lie. And clearly he had taken her silence as acquiescence because his head had descended and he made a harsh sound in his throat as he covered her mouth with his.

He was not gentle like before, when she had been half-asleep. This time his mouth moved over hers with total certainty, demanding her response and forcing her lips apart so that he could push his tongue between them. His fierce passion was shockingly primitive. Darcey felt overwhelmed by his potent masculinity. He evoked a level of need in her that she had not known she was capable of feeling—and, terrifyingly, she could not control it or subdue it.

She caught her breath as Salvatore slipped his hand inside her blouse and cupped her breast. The heat of his skin scorched through the sheer lace bra which offered no protection when he flicked his thumb-pad across the taut peak of her nipple. She could not restrain a soft cry as desire arrowed through her. Molten heat pooled between her legs and she squeezed her trembling thighs together in an attempt to ease the tense throb of her arousal.

Nothing had prepared her for the intensity of sexual hunger that swept through her. She had only had one lover. Marcus had teased her about the fact that she had been a virgin until she met him, but she had wanted to wait for her soulmate. She had thought she had found him. Making love with her husband had been enjoyable, although not earth-shattering, she admitted. Certainly with Marcus she had never felt this wild, wanton urgency to have sex that Salvatore was making her feel.

Everything faded and she was conscious only of Salvatore's mouth on hers as he deepened the kiss and it became incredibly erotic. Darcey responded to him help-lessly, utterly captivated by this stern-faced man, this dark stranger who, inexplicably, she felt she had been waiting for all her life. She ran her hands over his chest and felt the thunderous beat of his heart before she moved lower and traced the hard ridges of his abdominal mus-cles. Driven by instinct, she pulled his shirt from the waistband of his trousers and slid her fingers beneath the material to skim over his naked torso, loving the sensa-tion of his satin skin overlaid with rough hair.

Salvatore made a guttural sound when he felt Darcey's fingers drift over his abdomen. Her touch was as soft as a butterfly's wings on his sensitised flesh, and just imag-ining her stroking his manhood with her delicate fingers was making him hard. He was desperate to guide his throbbing shaft between her soft thighs and lose him-self in her sensual heat. Why not enjoy a few moments of carnal pleasure before he had to face the pain of his old friend's death?

He brought his mouth down on hers once more, crush-ing her lips that parted obligingly so that he could ex-plore her inner sweetness with his tongue. He could not remember ever feeling this out of control. His hunger for her consumed him, made him forget everything as he fo-cused on the feel of her silky skin when he eased her bra cups aside and caressed her naked breasts. The sight of her dusky pink nipples jutting provocatively forward was an irresistible temptation, but as he lowered his mouth to one taut peak a muffled sound pierced Salvatore's con-sciousness. It was little more than a soft murmur from the adjoining room, but it catapulted him back to reality.

Rosa!

He snatched his hands from Darcey's body. *Dio!* What the hell was he doing? What if his daughter had walked in? He sat up and raked an unsteady hand through his hair, breathing hard as he fought to bring his body under control.

It was fundamentally wrong for him to make love to Darcey when he could not remember his wife, whom presumably he had loved, he thought with savage self-contempt. He could never move forward with his life until he regained his memory and discovered what had happed in the accident that had resulted in his wife's death.

He glanced at Darcey and his jaw clenched when he saw that her lips were reddened and slightly swollen from his hungry passion. His gut ached with unfulfilled desire and he sprang up from the bed before he betrayed himself and pulled her beneath him.

'This should not have happened.'

He caught the stunned expression in her eyes and felt a flash of guilt when her bottom lip quivered and she bit down hard on the soft flesh. Her hand shook as she pulled her bra into place, and Salvatore tore his eyes from the sight of her pebble-hard nipples visible through the sheer fabric.

'I should not have kissed you,' he said harshly. 'I'm sorry.'

Darcey watched Salvatore stride over to the door, her disbelief that he had stopped kissing her rapidly turning to humiliation. She did not know why he had suddenly torn his mouth from hers, but the look of self-disgust she had seen in his eyes had doused her desire as swiftly as if she had plunged into an ice bath. He had kissed her senseless and aroused her until she was trembling with need, but now he was walking away from her and he was *sorry*! Thoughts swirled around her mind. Why had he stopped? Had he suddenly discovered that he did he not find her attractive or exciting?

She remembered how Marcus had complained that he wished she was more adventurous. She had naively believed he was satisfied with their love life, but according to her ex-husband she had been boring in bed. No doubt his mistress with the over-inflated chest had been a sexual gymnast, Darcey thought bitterly. Maybe that was what all men wanted, and maybe Salvatore had been disappointed with her.

He paused in the doorway and swung round. She saw his gaze flick to her gaping blouse. Blushing hotly, she yanked the edges together to hide her aroused body from his narrowed gaze.

'I hope you will agree that we cannot allow what just happened to affect our arrangement for you to stay here and give my daughter speech therapy. For her sake the best thing we can do is forget the incident,' he said brusquely, as if the 'incident' was something he could easily dismiss from his mind. 'I give you my assurance that it will not happen again.'

Salvatore strode through the connecting door to Rosa's bedroom, leaving Darcey gritting her teeth. Damned right it wouldn't happen again, she thought grimly. She would not risk making a fool of herself for a second time, or give him the chance to reject her as he had just done. He might be able to dismiss what had happened, but there was no chance she would forget, and for that reason her only option was to leave the castle and return to London.

Through the half-open door she watched him pause by the bed and bend down to pick up a teddy bear from the floor. He placed the bear on the pillow beside Rosa and then, to Darcey's surprise, leaned over and gently kissed the little girl's brow before he tucked the covers around her and walked out of the bedroom.

As soon as he had gone Darcey jumped up from the

bed, with the intention of packing the suitcase she had only unpacked a few hours earlier. But the memory of the tender expression she had witnessed on Salvatore's face when he had kissed his sleeping daughter lingered in her mind. Darcey felt certain that he loved Rosa, but for some reason he could not connect with his child or show her how much she meant to him. Perhaps it was a result of his own childhood. It sounded as though he had not had a close relationship with either of his parents.

She walked into the other room and looked at Rosa's innocent little face. If the little girl could speak, would that somehow help her to develop a closer relationship with her father? Darcey bit her lip, torn between never wanting to see Salvatore again and her conscience, which would not allow her to walk away from his motherless daughter. If she could encourage Salvatore to become involved in Rosa's speech therapy perhaps he would bond with his child and show her the love that she so clearly wanted.

Darcey sighed. She had always had a soft heart. As a child she had frequently rescued stray dogs and injured wildlife—memorably a hedgehog which, to her mother's horror, had been covered in fleas. Her brother had used to tease her that she could not save the world. But in this instance she had the expertise to help a deaf little girl.

She bit her lip as she recalled the grim expression on Salvatore's face when he had abruptly snatched his mouth from hers. Her common sense told her to leave before she became any deeper involved, but her heart was telling her something else.

A heat haze shimmered over the white tiles surrounding the pool and Darcey insisted on applying sunscreen to Rosa when she came out of the water. The memory of her mother's melanoma emphasised the importance of taking care in the sun.

Rosa had taken off her external listening device while she had been swimming, but once she had attached it again Darcey spoke and signed simultaneously to her. 'You're a very good swimmer. You're like a little fish.'

Rosa giggled. It was lovely to hear her laughing, Darcey thought, feeling a surge of affection for the little girl. She only wished that Salvatore was here to spend time with his daughter. The butler, Armond, had informed her at breakfast that Salvatore had gone out and would be away from the castle all day. Darcey had felt relieved that she did not have face him after what had happened the previous night, but Rosa had clearly been disappointed by her father's absence, and to cheer her up Darcey had offered to take her swimming.

Armond spoke good English and had explained that the pool was a new addition to the castle grounds that Salvatore had commissioned a year ago. Darcey had been startled to discover that the pool was heart-shaped. Recalling Lydia's statement that Salvatore had not come to terms with his wife's death, she wondered if he had chosen the shape of the pool as a declaration of his love for Adriana.

'Have you finished swimming?' she asked Rosa.

The little girl shook her head and pointed towards the far end of the pool area, where a young boy was hurtling towards them, followed by a tall man whose features bore a striking resemblance to Salvatore's and a heavily pregnant woman with long hair the colour of ripe corn.

'Nico, be careful!' the woman called as the little boy ran to the edge of the pool. She gave Darcey a rueful look. 'My son is such a daredevil. I just hope his new brother or sister won't be quite such a handful. I'm Kristen, by the way, and this is my husband, Sergio.'

She smiled at the handsome man at her side, her face radiantly beautiful. Darcey caught her breath as she observed the look of love that passed between the two of them. Sergio Castellano patently adored his wife, and Darcey felt a pang of wistful longing to be loved so utterly and unconditionally.

Sergio held out his hand. 'You must be Darcey. My brother told me you have come to Sicily to give Rosa speech therapy.' He gave an easy smile. 'If you can persuade her out of the pool! My niece is a real water baby.'

Darcey watched Rosa dive into the water. 'She's an amazingly good swimmer for such a young child.'

'Salvatore taught her. Swimming is good physiotherapy for his leg, and he took Rosa into the water with him from when she was a baby. He had this pool built for her—' He broke off. '*Nico*, don't go to the deep end until I'm with you.' Sergio laughed and pulled off his tee shirt. 'I'd better go in the pool and keep an eye on these two.'

Darcey stared at the heart-shaped pool. 'So Salvatore *does* love Rosa,' she murmured beneath her breath.

'Yes, he does. But, like you, I wasn't sure how he felt about his daughter when I first met him,' Kristen said quietly. 'The Castellano men find it hard to show their emotions.' A fleeting sadness crossed her lovely face. 'For a long time I didn't know that Sergio loved me, but thankfully we were able to work through the problems in our relationship. Both the brothers had difficult childhoods and were badly affected when their mother and father split up.'

'I suppose being sent away to boarding school when they were young didn't help,' Darcey commented.

'Sergio didn't go to school with Salvatore.' Kristen

hesitated. 'The brothers were separated when they were five years old.' She did not give any more details and lowered herself into a chair with a heartfelt sigh. 'Two weeks until the baby is due! I feel like an elephant, but Sergio insists that pregnancy suits me.'

'You look lovely,' Darcey assured her truthfully.

'Thank you.' Kristen gave her a friendly smile. 'I know it will be worth it in the end. Sergio is so excited about the baby, and it will be nice for Nico.' She sighed. 'It's a shame that Salvatore hasn't met anyone else. I think Rosa would love to have a mother, and perhaps a little brother or sister. But since Adriana's death Salvatore shuts himself away in his castle. He rarely leaves the estate, and all he focuses on is the vineyards and making wine. He has gone to the village chapel today to arrange the funeral of the head vintner. It's such a tragedy that Pietro died while he was attempting to save some of the wine. The old man was a good friend of Salvatore's.'

'I knew that some of the workers were injured in the fire, but I didn't realise someone had actually died.' Darcey felt guilty as she recalled how she had accused Salvatore of putting work before Rosa. How terrible that he had lost a friend in the fire.

'Salvatore is coming now.' Kristen shielded her eyes from the sun with her hand as she looked across the fields at a horse and rider galloping towards them. She sighed. 'I bet his leg will be painful after he's been riding. I'm a physiotherapist,' she explained. 'I've advised Salvatore that horse-riding overstretches the damaged muscles in his thigh, but he doesn't care. He's determined not to allow his injury to change the way he lives his life.' She gave Darcey a rueful smile. 'Be warned: the Castellano men can be very stubborn.'

Darcey watched the horse and rider thundering across

the field towards them. The horse's powerful flanks glistened with sweat and its mahogany-coloured mane streamed behind like a flag. The rider was no less impressive. Dressed entirely in black, with a bandana tied around his head to keep back the dark hair that fell around his shoulders, Salvatore looked like a pirate—ruthless, dangerous, and so devastatingly sexy that Darcey's heart thudded.

He dismounted and walked through the gate to the pool area, moving with an innate grace despite the stiffness in his right leg. Darcey felt herself blush and was aware that Kristen was looking curiously at her. Terrified that she might betray the effect Salvatore had on her, she jumped up and mumbled, 'I'll go and help Sergio with the children.'

As she walked down the steps into the pool her eyes were drawn to Salvatore, who greeted his sister-in-law with one of his rare smiles. Fortunately the water cooled Darcey's heated skin, and she concentrated on playing with Rosa and Nico, but she was conscious of Salvatore's penetrating gaze every time she darted him a glance.

Eventually Sergio called a halt to the swimming session and he and Kristen shepherded the children into the changing cubicles. Realising that she would have to wait for a cubicle, Darcey had no choice but to walk back to the sun lounger where she had left her towel—which happened to be where Salvatore had sat down.

'Rosa looked as though she was having fun.'

His gravelly voice did strange things to Darcey's insides. She blushed as she remembered in vivid detail the passion that had flared between them, and against her will her eyes were drawn to him. He looked incredibly sexy, with his swarthy complexion and a day's growth of dark stubble shading his jaw. His shirt was half-open, and the sight of his bare bronzed chest covered with wiry black hair evoked a flood of warmth between her thighs. She felt acutely self-conscious in her bikini, especially when she felt her nipples harden in response to Salvatore's devastating virility.

'I hope you don't mind that I brought Rosa swimming. I guessed you would be busy today.' She recalled Kristen saying that one of the winery workers had died in the fire. 'I'm sorry that your head vintner lost his life.'

'The funeral will take place tomorrow.' Salvatore's jaw clenched.

Darcey's gentle sympathy undermined his iron control over his emotions and he felt an inexplicable need to hold her in his arms and allow her sweet nature to ease his pain.

'Pietro was an excellent vintner who taught me everything I know about winemaking, and he was an even better friend,' he said gruffly. 'Thank you for looking after Rosa. I watched you playing with her in the pool and she clearly enjoys being with you.'

Darcey bit her lip. 'I realise that she could grow attached to me, and I to her. I have been thinking that I should go home and you should appoint another speech therapist.'

His dark brows lowered. 'Why do you want to leave?'

She flushed. 'Well, in light of what happened last night…I'm afraid it will be awkward for me to stay.'

Her wariness was understandable after his behaviour last night, Salvatore thought grimly. He should not have come on to her the way he had. But the passion that had exploded between them had been mutual, he reminded himself. Darcey had wanted him as much as he had wanted her. It was imperative for Rosa's sake that he persuaded Darcey to remain at the castle, but his daughter's need for speech therapy was not the only reason he hoped she would stay, he acknowledged.

'I do not see why it should be awkward. You are here in your professional capacity. The fact that there's a spark between us is immaterial. It happens between men and women all the time. I am sure we are both mature enough to be able to ignore an inconvenient attraction.' His eyes narrowed on her face. 'But perhaps there is another reason why you want to leave. Since your divorce there must have been other men in your life. Is there a lover back in England whom you are missing?'

'*No,*' Darcey said fiercely. 'I wouldn't have kissed you if I had a…a boyfriend.' She coloured hotly, thinking how naive she must sound. But she believed strongly in fidelity. It was a pity that Marcus had not shared her values, she thought wryly.

She dropped her gaze from Salvatore. The air around the pool was hot and still, broken only by the song of the cicadas in the bougainvillaea bushes.

'Why did your marriage end?' he asked abruptly.

She shrugged. 'We discovered that we weren't compatible. But the nail in the coffin of our relationship was when I discovered Marcus in bed with another woman.'

The moment the words were out Darcey regretted revealing something so personal and still so painful. She was over Marcus, but he had left her with a host of insecurities that Salvatore had opened up when he had rejected her the previous night. She looked away from him, hoping he would drop the conversation.

Salvatore watched Darcey gnaw her bottom lip with her teeth and felt an irrational rush of anger towards Marcus Rivers. From the moment he had introduced Darcey to his daughter he had been impressed by her kindness. Her soft heart did not deserve to be broken.

'The guy was obviously a jerk,' he said quietly.

Darcey bent her head so that her hair swung forward to partially hide her face. Her breath hitched in her throat as Salvatore lifted his hand and tucked a few strands behind her ear. His soft voice was unexpected and tugged on emotions she'd thought she had buried.

'I suppose it wasn't Marcus's fault that I'm not…' She flushed. 'That I didn't…excite him.'

'What do you mean?'

Oh, Lord, why had she started along this route? Darcey sighed. 'I'm hardly a sex siren. Marcus likes voluptuous women, and I'm not very well endowed in that department—as you no doubt noticed last night.'

For a few seconds Salvatore did not follow her, but as he stared into her eyes and recognised self-doubt, understanding dawned.

'What I noticed last night, and from the moment I first met you, is that you are very beautiful. How can you not know how lovely you are?' he asked intently when she looked disbelieving. 'You have a gorgeous figure.' An image flashed into his mind of her small, firm breasts with their pink, tightly puckered nipples. 'I've never been so turned on as I was last night,' he admitted roughly.

Darcey shot him a startled look. 'Then why did you stop…?'

'I heard Rosa make a sound, and I was concerned that she might wake up.'

It was the partial truth. Hearing his daughter had released Salvatore from Darcey's sensual spell and forced him back to cold reality. He was not free to make love to her while his amnesia continued to conceal his past. *Dio*, it was his fault that Adriana had died and Rosa was growing up without a mother. His guilt was a poison inside him and he did not want to taint Darcey with the blackness in his heart.

His eyes roamed her slender figure in a yellow bikini that was all the more sexy because it wasn't overtly revealing and desire knotted his stomach. She was so lovely, but she could not be his, and it was only fair that he should put some distance between them.

He stood up and began to walk away from her. 'We have agreed to ignore the attraction between us, and it will be best for Rosa if we stick to that arrangement,' he said curtly. 'I have some work to do in the vineyards and I might not get back to the castle until late. Armond will serve you dinner at eight o'clock.'

CHAPTER SIX

AT FIVE TO EIGHT Darcey walked into the dining room and felt her heart perform a somersault when she saw Salvatore standing by the window, his powerful frame silhouetted against the golden sunset. She had half expected him not to be back for dinner, and the sight of him shook her composure.

The bandana had gone, and he had changed out of jeans and riding boots into tailored black trousers and a collarless white shirt made of such fine silk that she could see the shadow of his dark chest hair through it. She was aware of her body's instant reaction to him—the way her nipples tingled and sprang to attention—and was thankful that the chiffon shawl which matched her dress hid the evidence of his effect on her.

'Good evening, Darcey.' Salvatore's hard-boned face showed no expression, but his eyes narrowed as he swept his gaze over her, taking in her slender figure in a jade-coloured jersey-silk dress. He wondered why she was hugging her shawl around her like a security blanket. 'Lydia will be joining us for dinner—but she is usually late,' he said wryly. 'Can I get you a drink while we wait?'

Dismissing the temptation to have something strong and alcoholic, hopefully to dull her senses and her fierce awareness of him, Darcey instead asked for fruit juice. She had no option but to walk across the room to him, but when he handed her a glass of pomegranate juice she moved over to the window to watch the dying rays of the sun streak the sky blood-red. Above the castle's highest tower the dark shadow of an eagle circled. Even from a distance Darcey could see that it was holding something in its hooked beak. Probably a mouse or a rabbit that it had just killed, she thought, and a shiver ran down her spine. There was a ruthless cruelty to the rugged landscape that she sensed suited the mood of the master of Torre d'Aquila.

Salvatore reminded himself that he deserved Darcey's coolness. But he missed her bright smile. After he had left her by the pool he had visited the mortuary for a final time to pay his respects to Pietro and had felt the unfamiliar sting of tears in his eyes. He had not cried since he was a small boy, when his father had told him his mother had left and would not be coming back.

His headache had begun soon after he had left the mortuary and now throbbed dully behind his temples. His consultant had explained that in some amnesia cases the sufferer's memory returned suddenly. His startling insight that Adriana had disliked living at the castle had given him hope that the past was about to reveal itself to him. But to his frustration a black curtain still obscured his memory.

His savage mood was not improved by the company of his mother-in-law. Lydia arrived twenty minutes late for dinner and spent the entire meal talking about Adriana.

'The birth of their child cemented my daughter's relationship with Salvatore,' Lydia told Darcey. 'It was just a pity that Rosa turned out to be flawed.'

Darcey frowned. 'How do you mean, flawed?'

'Well, the fact that she's deaf and dumb.' Lydia sniffed. 'Her defective hearing doesn't come from *our* side of the family. Adriana had perfect hearing.'

'Rosa's deafness has nothing to do with a genetic link.'

Darcey had not taken to Lydia when she had first met her, and now she felt a surge of dislike for the woman. She had hoped that Rosa's grandmother would support the little girl through speech therapy, but when she had spoken to Lydia before dinner and mentioned that she might like to take part in therapy sessions Lydia had refused, saying that she would be bored.

'Rosa is a very intelligent child, and I have no doubt that she will learn to speak very quickly,' she told Lydia firmly. 'But it is crucial that she has encouragement from her family.'

She looked across the table at Salvatore. 'I've already explained that for speech therapy to be successful it must be continual, and I will incorporate it into Rosa's daily life. But I think she will benefit from an hour to an hour and a half of intensive therapy every day, which I would like you to attend. Afternoons would be best, and I thought that after the session you could take her swimming. It's something she loves and will look forward to.'

She held his gaze, challenging him to refuse her request.

'I realise that you will have to take time away from work, but Rosa needs your support.'

'And she will have it,' Salvatore assured her. He had been impressed by Darcey's fierce defence of Rosa and the way she had put Lydia in her place. 'Your idea of taking Rosa to the pool afterwards is a good one. I hope you will swim with us? I realise that you should be on your holiday, and I want you to have some relaxation time.'

The chances of her feeling relaxed around Salvatore

were zero, Darcey thought wryly. Just the idea of him wearing nothing but a pair of swim shorts made her feel hot and bothered. He had stated that it would be best if they ignored the chemistry they both felt, but his eyes sought hers and she felt as though she was drowning in his liquid dark gaze. Her awareness of her surroundings faded and she was aware only of Salvatore—master of his castle, a sorcerer who had trapped her in his sensual spell.

Shaken by the simmering sexual tension between them, she unconsciously lifted her hand to the pendant around her neck and traced the four-leaf clover, taking comfort from its familiar shape and the reminder of her father who had given it to her. Home and her family seemed a long way away, and she wished fervently that she was in France at the villa at Le Lavandou, where she had spent so many happy family holidays.

'Oh!' She stared at the pendant in her hand and re-alised that the chain had broken.

'That's the trouble with cheap jewellery.' Lydia's voice broke the silence and released Darcey from Salvatore's bewitchment. 'It's a pretty trinket, I'll grant you, but peridots aren't particularly valuable.'

Darcey placed the necklace on the tablecloth. 'It has sentimental value.'

Lydia shrugged. 'The engagement ring that Salvatore gave to Adriana is a ten-carat diamond solitaire. After her death I kept it as a memento of my darling.' She looked at Salvatore. 'Adriana told me you proposed to her at a five-star hotel in Rome. It must have been *so* romantic.'

Salvatore's jaw tightened as he glanced up at the wall, where another photograph of his wife hung at his mother-in-law's request. No memory came to him of when he had proposed to Adriana. He stared at the picture, will-ing the curtain blocking his mind to open. How could he not remember the woman who, according to Lydia, he had adored? he wondered grimly. Was his love so fickle that it could so easily be forgotten? Or was he flawed, emotionally deficient and unable to love deeply—or be loved? Frustration surged up inside him and he jerked to his feet, conscious of the surprised looks from Darcey and Lydia.

'Excuse me,' he growled.

As he strode out of the dining room it occurred to him that usually when he was in a black mood he would visit Pietro. His old friend had always known how to calm him. But Pietro was dead. He thought briefly of going to see his father. Recently there had been a *rapprochement* between him and Tito, helped by Sergio who, since his marriage to Kristen, had become closer to their father. But Tito was in poor health and went to bed early. He did not want to disturb his brother. Sergio had enough to worry about with the imminent birth of his second child.

When had he ever needed anyone? Salvatore asked himself mockingly. All his life he had felt alone, and he did not understand why tonight he longed for the company of a girl with green eyes and a sweet smile that made his guts ache.

Darcey entered her bedroom and closed the door with a sigh of relief. After Salvatore had abruptly walked out of the dining room halfway through dinner his mother-in-law had spent the rest of the evening talking incessantly about her daughter. Adriana had apparently been a paragon of beauty and sophistication.

'My late husband, Adriana's father, was an Italian count,' Lydia had explained. 'He was much older than me and he died when Adriana was a child. But it is evident in her photographs that she was of noble blood.'

It was little wonder that Salvatore had been so deeply in love with Adriana, Lydia had said. Considering that the castle was filled with photographs of the beautiful brunette, Darcey guessed that Lydia was right and Salvatore was still mourning his wife. She frowned as she recalled that several times during their conversation Lydia had hinted that Salvatore felt guilty about Adriana's death. But why on earth should he? she wondered. She did not actually know how his wife had died. That was another mystery hidden within the castle's thick walls.

Someone had turned back the covers on the bed and the crisp white sheets looked inviting. Yawning, Darcey slipped off her shawl, but as she went to take off her necklace she remembered that the chain had broken at dinner and the pendant must still be on the dining table where she had left it.

The stone floors echoed beneath her feet as she hurried back downstairs, but when she walked into the dining room her heart sank as she saw that the table had been cleared. The butler was standing by a cabinet, polishing a silver candleholder. He looked round when he heard Darcey's footsteps.

'Armond, I left a necklace on the table.'

'*Sì.*' He nodded. 'Signore Castellano found it and took it with him.'

'Thank you.'

Why had Salvatore walked out during dinner? Darcey mused as she retraced her steps back upstairs. Had Lydia's constant references to Adriana been too painful? She knew his room was along the corridor from hers, and when she walked past she saw a light filtering beneath the door. Anxious to retrieve her pendant, she hesitated for a few seconds and then knocked.

Moments later the door opened and Salvatore's powerful frame filled the opening. His shirt was partially undone, and Darcey's eyes were drawn to the exposed bronzed skin overlaid with black chest hair.

'Darcey?'

His deep, sensual voice sent a shiver of awareness through her. She swallowed. 'Armond said you have my necklace?'

'I was trying to mend the broken clasp.' He opened the door wider. 'Come in while I finish the repair.'

The master suite's large sitting room was simply furnished, almost austere, with its rough plastered walls covered with faded tapestries that Darcey guessed were as old as the castle. The antique sofas had scrolled arms and rich blue brocade cushions which matched the rug that lay on top of the polished floorboards. Through a half-open door she could see that the bedroom was dominated by a huge four-poster bed with brocade drapes, and a brick fireplace that was so tall she could practically stand in the recess. She wondered if the castle had a modern heating system, or if in the winter a fire would blaze in the hearth. Now a vase of sunflowers stood in the grate and provided a bold splash of colour.

Quickly looking away from the bed, she moved across to the table, where her necklace lay next to some delicate-looking tools.

'I use these instruments to repair the clocks in the castle,' Salvatore explained. 'There are over a hundred clocks. All of them are incredibly old, and none actually keep the right time,' he said wryly.

'Why do you keep them, then?'

He shrugged. 'They belong here.'

Just as Salvatore belonged at Torre d'Aquila, Darcey thought. Tonight he reminded her more than ever of a knight from a previous century: a fearless warrior with an impressive physique that made her feel weak at the knees when she imagined his strong arms around her, crushing her against his broad chest as he ravaged her mouth with demanding passion.

She let out her breath on a shaky sigh, wishing she had never entered his room, but as she reached to take her necklace he scooped it up.

'I've adjusted the clasp and it should fasten securely now. Turn around and lift up your hair.'

Darcey's heart thudded as she turned away from him and gathered her hair in one hand to expose her neck. Salvatore draped the necklace around her so that the pendant rested in the valley between her breasts. She held her breath while he fastened the chain's clasp. His warm breath stirred the tendrils of hair at her nape and her heart beat faster. Why was he taking so long?

'Your skin is so pale and soft,' he murmured as he skimmed his hand along the line of her slender shoulder. 'You said the necklace holds sentimental value? Is that because it reminds you of your marriage?'

Darcey remembered that she had told him her father had given her the four-leaf-clover pendant to wish her good luck on her wedding day.

'Why would you want a reminder of the jerk who hurt you?' Salvatore said roughly. 'Are you still in love with him?'

'Of course not.' Darcey swallowed, certain that she had felt Salvatore's lips briefly brush against her neck. Her common sense told her to run from his room, but her feet seemed to be stuck to the floor. 'My feelings for the necklace have nothing to do with Marcus. I love it because it was a gift from my father. It once belonged to his mother, who he was very close to, and I was touched that he chose to give the pendant to me.'

She felt another fleeting caress on her bare shoulder and her stomach muscles clenched with sexual longing.

'Did you have a happy childhood?'

'Very.' Despite her father's unpredictable and sometimes difficult nature, Darcey knew that Joshua cared deeply for his children. 'My family mean the world to me.'

'You are fortunate.' Abruptly Salvatore dropped his hands and stepped away from her. 'My childhood memories are not so happy.'

'Kristen said that you were separated from your twin brother when you were young. Why did your parents decide to do that?'

'When my mother left my father she snatched Sergio and took him to America, but she left me behind. I don't know why,' Salvatore added, anticipating Darcey's next question. 'I grew up believing that she loved my brother but not me. Recently Sergio revealed that our mother beat him when he was a child. She had a problem with alcohol and he bore the brunt of her violent mood swings.'

He gave a humourless laugh when he saw her shocked expression.

'I guess I was lucky that she abandoned me. I was never subjected to physical abuse. In fact I rarely saw my father. I was away in England for long periods of time, but my boarding school was not an unpleasant place, and at least I learned to be self-sufficient from an early age.'

Love had been the missing factor from Salvatore's upbringing, Darcey mused, and she was sure it was the reason he found it difficult to connect on an emotional level with his daughter. But presumably he must have had a loving relationship with his wife. According to Lydia, Salvatore and Adriana's marriage had been blissfully happy, despite Lydia's vague hints that Salvatore was somehow responsible for Adriana's death.

Troubled by her conversation with Lydia, Darcey suddenly felt chilled as she glanced at Salvatore. He had moved across the room and was sitting on a stone window seat that had been hewn out of the castle walls. The curtains were open, revealing the black night sky, and the moon gleamed with cold brilliance and cast shadows over his hard-boned face.

Uncovering Salvatore's past might help her to understand him better, and perhaps give her an insight into how she could help him bond with Rosa.

Taking a deep breath, Darcey asked softly, 'How did Adriana die?'

For what seemed an age he did not answer, and when he did finally turn to face her his expression was unfathomable.

'I killed her.'

'What…what do you mean?' She was sure she could not have heard him correctly. Instinctively she crossed her arms in front of her as a shiver ran down her spine.

Something flashed in his dark eyes—a momentary glint of emotion that disappeared before she could define it.

'Adriana died when the car we were travelling in crashed down a mountainside.' Salvatore's jaw clenched. 'I was driving. We were both thrown out of an open-topped sports car. Adriana was pronounced dead at the scene of the accident. I regained consciousness a few days later to the news that I had lost my wife and there was a good chance I would lose my leg. Obviously my injuries, serious though they were, did not compare with the fact that Adriana had been killed,' he said grimly. 'It is entirely my fault that a young woman had her life cut cruelly short, and my fault that my daughter is growing up without her mother.'

The torment in his eyes made Darcey's heart ache, and without thinking about what she was doing she hurried across the room to stand in front of him.

'It was an accident—a terrible tragedy, but still an accident,' she told him intently. 'Sometimes events happen and we can't understand the reason for them.' She placed her hand on his arm, instinctively trying to offer him the comfort of contact with another human being. 'Do you know why you lost control of the car? Perhaps it was raining and you skidded?'

'What a soft heart you have, Darcey,' Salvatore said mockingly. He looked down at her pale hand, lying on his tanned forearm, and lifted his own hand to cup her chin. 'Why are you so determined to find excuses for me? Nothing can absolve me and I can never forgive myself for causing my wife's death.' He shrugged. 'Perhaps there were extenuating circumstances that had some bearing on the crash. I don't know because I don't remember.'

'Do you mean you suffered memory loss due to the crash?'

'I have no memory of the accident, or much of my life before it. I can't remember Adriana.' He stared into Darcey's shocked eyes. 'Since the accident I have had amnesia. I don't remember a goddamned thing about my marriage—or the love I felt for my wife.'

Darcey's head was reeling from the dramatic revelations of the past few minutes. 'You must have loved her,' she said shakily.

She unconsciously clasped Salvatore's arm tighter. His hard features were no longer expressionless. He looked haunted. The man behind the mask was finally exposed, and the burden of being unable to remember the car crash that had had such devastating consequences was reflected in his tortured eyes.

'There are photographs of Adriana everywhere in the castle,' Darcey said. 'Last night at dinner when you looked at her picture I assumed you were thinking of how much you missed her. '

'Lydia put the pictures up. I look at them, hoping they will jog my memory, but nothing comes. It's as if my mind is blocked by an impenetrable wall that hides the recent past from me. I can recall my childhood, but nothing of how I met Adriana, our wedding day—or, worst of all, Rosa's birth. Sometimes I look at my daughter and I feel that she is a stranger,' Salvatore admitted with raw honesty.

'Oh, that's awful.' Darcey bit her lip.

Salvatore's words explained why he shunned a close relationship with Rosa, and the real tragedy was that both father and daughter were suffering because of his memory loss.

'Isn't there something you could do to try to bring your memory back? Some form of psychotherapy?'

'Do you think I haven't tried?' he said roughly. 'I've met numerous psychoanalysts and they all say the same thing—that I have to be patient and hope that in time my memory will return. But no one can guarantee that I will *ever* regain my memory.' He frowned. 'When we arrived at the castle I experienced a flashback. You had just asked me if Adriana liked living here and I remembered that she hadn't. She found the place too remote and quiet. But I don't know how or why I know that.' His voice was taut with frustration. 'I hoped I would recall more about her, *feel* some sort of connection to her, but my mind is blank.

He tightened his grip on Darcey's chin and tilted her

head so that she was forced to meet his gaze. 'I assume
that I must have loved and desired my wife. But the truth
is I can't believe I ever felt the fierce desire for her that
I feel for you, *mia belleza*. Ever since I walked into your
office I have been burning up with wanting you, consumed with the need to kiss you...' his voice dropped
to a husky drawl that sent liquid heat coursing through
Darcey's veins '...make love to you.'

'You...you shouldn't say things like that.' She desperately tried to ignore the bolt of sexual excitement that
shot through her. Salvatore had moved so that she was
trapped between his legs, and because he was sitting on
the window seat her face was on level with his. She swallowed when she saw the sultry gleam in his eyes. 'We
agreed that I came here for Rosa's sake,' she whispered.

'What if I told you that I want you for *my* sake?' he
said thickly. 'What if I told you that I can't sleep at night
for thinking about you? Would your heart soften towards
me, sweet Darcey?'

She was mesmerised by the raw need in his voice,
shocked by the hunger that he made no effort to hide.
His desire for her acted as a panacea to the hurt and
humiliation she had felt when she had discovered Marcus's infidelity. Even so, her heart thudded with panic
when his arm snaked around her waist and he jerked
her towards him. She had never had casual sex before.
Perhaps it's time you started, whispered a wicked voice
inside her head.

A tremor ran through her as she watched Salvatore's
head descend, but her desire to flee from him was over-
ruled by a far more primitive desire to succumb to his
sensual mastery. Time seemed to be suspended. She
could hear her blood thundering in her ears, and from

outside in the darkness there came the harsh screech of an owl on its nightly hunt for prey.

At the last second her common sense urged her to pull away from him—but it was too late.

'Salvatore…don't—'

The rest of her words were obliterated as he slanted his mouth over hers. The firm pressure of his lips instantly enslaved her and she trembled as he slid his hand from her chin to her nape and angled her head so that he could plunder her mouth mercilessly.

She had not expected him to be gentle, but the force of his passion shocked and thrilled her.

'Open your mouth,' he demanded, and with a low moan she complied.

His answering groan of satisfaction as he probed his tongue between her lips shattered the last of her defences, and she cupped his face in her hands and kissed him back with fierce urgency.

He had told her he was consumed with need, and now Darcey understood as molten heat surged through her veins and the ache low in her pelvis became an insistent throb. The rights or wrongs of making love with a man she barely knew no longer mattered. In a strange way she felt that she had been waiting for Salvatore all her life.

He trailed his mouth over her throat and along the fragile line of her collarbone. Darcey caught her breath when he slid the strap of her dress over her shoulder and her heart slammed against her ribcage as he peeled the top of her dress down, lower and lower, until he had bared her breast. Her nipple reacted instantly to the brush of his fingers. His warm breath teased her senses and she could not restrain a soft cry as he flicked his tongue over the dusky peak he had exposed.

'*Santa Madonna!* You are so beautiful,' Salvatore said

hoarsely. 'I took one look at you in your prim suit and I imagined doing this.'

He proceeded to demonstrate what he had imagined doing by drawing her nipple into his mouth and tugging gently, causing a shaft of pleasure to arc from Darcey's breasts to her pelvis. She trembled as he curled his fingers possessively around her other breast, and felt impatient for him to strip off her dress completely so that he could caress her naked flesh.

'You know how this is going to end, *cara*?'

His voice was thick with sexual tension and the glitter in his eyes warned her of his intention to make love to her. It was what she wanted, Darcey acknowledged. In fact she would surely die if he did not take her to bed right now. But lingering doubts from her disastrous marriage to Marcus meant that she did not have the nerve to tell Salvatore that her need was as great as his. Instead she slid her hands behind his neck and pulled his mouth down to hers to initiate a kiss that was sweetly passionate.

Her clumsy eagerness touched something deep inside Salvatore. His conscience told him it was wrong to desire her when he was still chained to his hidden past. But he could not deny his need for her any longer. He stood up, intending to lift her into his arms and carry her through to the bedroom, but a sudden searing pain shot down his thigh. He grabbed hold of the bureau to prevent himself from falling and the porcelain vase standing on its polished surface fell to the floor, shattering into dozens of shards.

Darcey gave a startled cry. She stared at Salvatore, shocked that his eyes were no longer warm with sensual promise but hard and bitter. His face might have been carved from granite, but she had no idea what had caused his transformation from passionate lover to cold stranger.

'What's wrong?' she whispered.

Beads of sweat formed on Salvatore's brow as agonising pain ripped through his thigh. He knew there was nothing he could do but wait for the muscle spasms to ease. Until they did, walking was impossible.

The gentle concern in Darcey's eyes poisoned his soul. His Sicilian pride could not bear for her to witness his physical weakness. His jaw clenched. She was so beautiful. Even though she had pulled her dress back into place he pictured her small, firm breasts and his body ached with sexual need. But he could not make love to her now. The cramp in his leg was a timely reminder of the accident that he had been responsible for. He could not bear to see Darcey's expression when he took off his trousers and revealed the horrific mess of his scarred thigh. She might be revolted—or, even worse, she might feel sorry for him.

Darcey put her hand on Salvatore's arm, desperate to understand the torment in his eyes. 'Let me help you...'

Her sweetness brought bile to Salvatore's throat. He fought the temptation to hold her in his arms and accept the comfort she offered. He felt unmanned, and he channelled his pain into anger.

'You cannot help me,' he told her savagely.

The flare of hurt in her eyes almost stopped him, but the truth was that he was no good for her. His instincts told him that she was not very sexually experienced; certainly she was not like the casual mistresses he had from time to time, who understood that there was no possibility of him ever wanting a deeper relationship. He knew that Darcey was fascinated by him; he was aware of the way she watched him when she thought he did not notice. But he could never be the sort of man she hoped for or deserved.

He gripped her chin and brought her face close to his. 'I am not the man for you, sweet Darcey. You are curiously innocent, but there is a blackness in my soul that I fear would destroy you.'

He dropped a hard kiss on her mouth and his gut clenched when he felt her immediate response. He closed his eyes briefly and thrust her away from him.

'Get out. Run from me, Darcey. Because if you don't I will take your lovely body and crush your gentle heart.'

His eyes glittered when she did not move. The pain in his leg felt as though he was being stabbed with hot knives, but he compressed his mouth, determined not to let her see his weakness.

'Did you hear me?' he snarled. 'If you know what's good for you—g*et out*!'

Slowly, Darcey backed towards the door. She could hardly believe the transformation in Salvatore. A few moments ago he had wanted to make love to her, but now he clearly resented her presence. He was rejecting her—as her father sometimes still did when he was more interested in his work, and as her ex-husband had done when he'd discovered that marrying her had not helped his acting career. The two men she had loved in her life had both been disappointed with her, and now Salvatore was sending her away. But she did not know why he had changed his mind.

Mystery surrounded him. She sensed he was haunted by the fact that he could not remember the accident in which his wife had died. Perhaps his subconscious had stopped him from making love to her because he still loved Adriana. Darcey shivered. It was mortifying enough to think that Salvatore did not desire her, but even worse was the idea that while he had been kissing her he had imagined her to be the ghost of his dead wife.

To her shame, her body still ached with unfulfilled desire—but Salvatore's face was as hard as stone and the coldness in his black eyes was the final humiliation. Uttering a low cry, Darcey spun round and fled from the room.

CHAPTER SEVEN

TAORMINA WAS PERCHED high on the cliffs and offered spectacular views of the sea and the beach resorts of Mazzaro and Isola Bella. The town had a mixture of beautifully restored medieval buildings as well as modern shops, bars and restaurants which catered for the many tourists who came to explore the myriad winding streets. Darcey admired the varied architecture left behind by the Greeks, Romans and Byzantines, to name but a few of the conquering armies who had occupied Taormina in the past, but if she was honest she was just as impressed by the numerous boutiques and shoe shops.

Standing with her nose almost pressed against the glass, she couldn't decide whether she preferred the strappy tan leather sandals with a wedge heel or the eye-catching red shoes with four-inch stiletto heels.

Rosa tugged on her hand to gain her attention. *Which ones do you like?* she signed.

Darcey gave a rueful smile as she signed back, *All of them! But I don't need any more shoes.* She glanced up the street and her heart did a familiar flip when she saw Salvatore walking towards them. *Look, there's Papa*, she signed, and pointed him out to Rosa.

As he drew nearer she purposefully turned back to study the shoes displayed in the shop window. Two weeks had passed since the night she had fled from his room, and during that time they had treated each other with cool politeness—at least on the surface. Occasionally when she darted him a glance she glimpsed a flare of sexual desire in his eyes that evoked an ache of longing inside her. But pride made her resist showing any sign of warmth to him. She reminded herself that she had come to Sicily in her professional capacity and strove to focus on Rosa, trying to ignore her inconvenient attraction to the little girl's father.

But, although she did everything she could to avoid him at the castle, she could not stop thinking about his situation and in particular his difficult relationship with Rosa. She had come to the conclusion that until Salvatore recovered from his amnesia he would never be able to move forward with his life or be able to bond with his daughter. If only he could remember what had caused the car accident four years ago he might be able to forgive himself for Adriana's death. But his memory showed no sign of returning, and Darcey sensed his frustration.

She stiffened as she realised that he was standing behind her. The scent of sandalwood cologne teased her senses and she hated her body's treacherous reaction to him. Salvatore's problems were none of her business, Darcey reminded herself. She was determined to maintain an emotional and physical distance from him, but perversely, in the last few days, he seemed just as determined to engineer a thaw in their relationship. At dinner he had stopped being grim-faced and uncommunicative and had drawn her into conversation, asking about her work and her life in London. And today, to her surprise, he had joined her and Rosa for breakfast and suggested that they should spend the day in Taormina.

'Surely you don't need another pair of shoes?' he murmured now, and the gentle teasing in his voice tugged on Darcey's heart. 'I've seen you wear at least ten different pairs since you arrived in Sicily.'

Taking a deep breath, she pinned a cool smile on her face before spinning round to him. 'A woman can never have enough shoes. But I'm not going to buy any of these—they're too expensive.'

'Perhaps you will allow me to buy them for you?' Salvatore glanced at Rosa and signed, *Which shoes does Darcey like best?*

The little girl immediately responded—*The red ones.*

The joke had gone far enough. Darcey glared at him as he pulled out his wallet. 'Of course I won't let you buy me shoes. If you're so determined to spend money, Rosa has seen some pretty hairbands in the shop just along the street. Why don't you let her show them to you while I pop to the chemist?'

What he would like to do, Salvatore mused as he skimmed his eyes over Darcey's slender shape, in figure-hugging white pedal-pushers and a gingham blouse, was pull her into his arms and kiss her stubborn mouth until she melted. He was sick to death of her imitation of the Ice Queen from one of Rosa's storybooks, and the knowledge that he deserved her frostiness did nothing to lessen his frustration. None of his feelings showed on his face, however.

'Good idea,' he said steadily, and held out his hand to Rosa. 'We'll meet you at the café on the other side of the *piazza*.'

As Darcey walked along the street she refused to speculate on the change in Salvatore's attitude towards her. He had been easier to deal with when he had treated her with cold indifference, she thought ruefully. At least then she'd been able to pretend that she wasn't interested in him.

Her thoughts were distracted by the sound of a distinctive high-pitched voice and, glancing down a narrow alleyway, she was surprised to see Lydia talking to a man. Darcey had no wish to meet Salvatore's mother-in-law and was about to continue on her way. But she paused when she realised that Lydia and her companion were arguing. They were speaking in Italian, and Darcey could not understand what was being said, but it was clear that the conversation was heated. Several times she heard Lydia address the man as Ettore. They continued their discussion for several more minutes, and then, to Darcey's shock, Lydia burst into tears and rushed away.

What had all that been about? she wondered. Even more puzzling was the fact that Lydia was in town when she had made a point of telling Darcey that morning that she planned to spend the day at the castle.

She was still musing over the scene she had witnessed in the alleyway as she crossed the attractive black and white paving of the Piazza XI Aprile in the centre of Taormina. Rosa ran to meet her and excitedly showed off her new hair accessories.

'Did you get everything you needed?' Salvatore asked as they strolled towards a café.

'Yes.' Darcey hesitated. 'Do you know someone called Ettore? I saw Lydia talking with a man—well, they seemed to be arguing. She called him Ettore.'

'It might have been Ettore Varsi.' Salvatore frowned. 'Ettore was the first person to arrive at the scene of the accident four years ago. He was driving a little way behind me and saw me lose control of the car on a sharp bend. After the crash he managed to scramble down the mountainside and he pulled Adriana and I away from the wreckage seconds before the car caught fire. I don't know why Lydia might have been arguing with Ettore,'

Salvatore continued. 'Perhaps you misunderstood. Lydia has always been grateful to him for trying to save her daughter.' A bleak expression crossed his face.

'Have you discussed with Ettore what happed that night? If you spoke to him, something might trigger your memory...' Darcey's voice faltered when she saw the grimness in Salvatore's eyes.

'Ettore Varsi gave a full statement of the facts to the police and at Adriana's inquest,' he said curtly. 'He had been at the party which Adriana and I had attended, and he saw us leave. His evidence states that I got into the driver's seat of the car and Adriana into the passenger seat. He followed behind us and believed that I was driving too fast as I approached a bend in the road. According to Ettore, the car spun and crashed through the roadside barrier. He stopped and called the emergency services before he climbed down the mountainside to try to rescue us.'

'I still think you should talk to him,' Darcey insisted. 'He might know more...'

'Enough!' Salvatore said harshly. 'There *is* nothing more. Ettore explained what he saw. Nothing can exonerate me from the fact that I am responsible for my wife's death.'

Darcey stared at him in frustration. 'You're so stubborn.'

'Me! Look at yourself, *cara*. Take my advice and stop poking your nose where it doesn't belong.'

So furious that she did not trust herself to speak, Darcey spun round and stalked into the café where Rosa had found a vacant table. She only wanted to help, she thought hotly, but Salvatore had made it clear that he did not want anything from her. The memory of how he had ordered her to get out of his room was still horribly embarrassing and she vowed that from now on she would not talk to him about anything other than how Rosa's speech therapy was progressing—which, after all, was the only reason she had come to Sicily.

She ordered fruit juice for Rosa, a cappuccino for herself and an espresso for Salvatore—although she wondered if he would join them now that she had put him in one of his black moods. But to her surprise he was smiling when he walked into the café a few minutes later.

'I've just had a call from Sergio,' he told her. 'Kristen went into labour early this morning and gave birth to a healthy baby boy half an hour ago.'

'Oh, that's wonderful!' Darcey waited for Salvatore to sign the news to Rosa that she had a new cousin. 'Your brother must be so relieved,' she said, recalling how Sergio had become increasingly tense as his wife's due date had approached.

'He's overjoyed.' Salvatore glanced at the coffee in front of him. 'I think we should celebrate baby Leo Castellano's birth with champagne.'

'Rosa can't drink champagne,' Darcey pointed out. *Shall we have ice cream?* she signed to the little girl, and was rewarded with a smile and a fervent nod.

Salvatore passed on a sweet treat, but as he watched Darcey and his daughter enjoying ice cream sundaes he was struck yet again by the close friendship they had formed. Darcey's kindness was apparent in everything she did, and she made Rosa's speech therapy sessions full of fun. He knew she did not understand why he found it hard to bond with Rosa. How could she comprehend the guilt he felt that his child was growing up without a mother—just as he had done? His amnesia had created a barrier between him and Rosa. *Dio!* He could not even remember her birth, or holding his newborn daughter in his arms.

The blankness in his mind evoked blackness in his heart. He had been right to send Darcey away instead of making love to her, Salvatore told himself. He knew he had hurt her feelings, but it was better than dragging her into his dark world. He had no right to taint her bright smile and cheerful nature with his despair. One day she would meet a man who would love her as she deserved to be loved, and she would love him back with all the generosity in her heart.

In brooding silence Salvatore drank his coffee and noted with heavy irony that its bitter taste matched the bitterness of his thoughts.

'Okay, that's enough for today.' Darcey simultaneously spoke and signed to Rosa. She gathered up the phonetics cards they had been using and smiled at the little girl. 'Well done! You spoke all the sounds we've been practising perfectly. I'm very pleased with you, and so is your *papa*.' She glanced at Salvatore, silently willing him to praise Rosa.

He had been as good as his word and joined in the speech therapy sessions every afternoon, but although he appeared relaxed and gave plenty of encouragement, Darcey still sensed a faintly reserved air with his daughter. To her relief he gave one of his rare smiles.

'You did very well today,' he told Rosa. 'Go and get ready for swimming.'

Darcey had decided to hold the therapy sessions in the summerhouse by the pool, so that Rosa could have her reward of a swim with her father immediately afterwards. Salvatore watched her run off to the changing cubicle.

'She seems to be making good progress.'

'She certainly is,' Darcey assured him. 'I realised when I met Rosa that she is a very bright child, and I'm confident she will quickly develop speech and language skills.'

'Thanks to you and your skill and dedication.' Salvatore rested his brooding gaze on her flushed face. 'Are you going to join us in the pool today?'

He frowned when Darcey shook her head.

'I need to use the time that you swim with Rosa to get on with some work. There's a lot to do to set up my private speech therapy practice,' she explained.

The excuse was partly true, for she *had* been researching possible venues where she could run her business. But she also used her free time to study the role she was to portray in her father's play. Reading Joshua's script, Darcey was amazed by his great talent as a playwright. She was so proud of her father, and pleased that he chosen her for the lead role, but she was plagued by self-doubt, and for that reason she had decided not to tell anyone outside of her family that she was going to be in the play until she was certain she could justify her father's faith in her.

'Why don't you be honest?'

Salvatore's terse voice dragged Darcey from her thoughts.

'I know you are revolted by the sight of my scars, but you've watched me swimming with Rosa every day since you arrived here—surely you've had time to get used to the mess my leg is in by now?'

'I'm *not* revolted by your scars!' She was shocked by the conclusion he had come to about her refusal to join him in the pool. 'I just think it's important that you and Rosa spend some time together,' she insisted.

Salvatore's gaze held a momentary look of doubt before he walked off to get changed.

Darcey pulled up her father's script on her laptop and tried to focus. The play was set in the time of the Second World War and was based on a true story about Joshua's mother, Edith, who had married a Frenchman and worked with the French Resistance until she was caught by the Nazis and tortured. Amazingly, Edith had managed to escape and had returned to Ireland, where her husband had later joined her, and the couple had gone on to have five children.

It was an inspiring story, and Joshua Hart's play was a moving tribute to his mother's bravery. But Darcey could not concentrate when her eyes were drawn to the pool. The sight of Salvatore's bronzed, athletic body proved a major distraction. It was true that the deep scars on his thigh were unmissable, but they certainly did not lessen the impact of his potent virility. He was the sexiest man she had ever met and Darcey gave a heavy sigh as she forced her eyes back to her laptop screen.

The sound of footsteps on the decking of the summerhouse made her look up, and she was surprised to see Rosa standing in front of her. The little girl took a deep breath.

'Dar-cey!' she said clearly.

'Oh, Rosa—you clever girl!' Darcey's eyes filled with tears of emotion that Rosa had spoken her first word. It was a breakthrough moment and she threw her arms around the child and hugged her.

'She has been practising saying your name with me,' Salvatore explained as he joined them in the summerhouse. 'Rosa is hoping that you will swim with us.'

Darcey gave him a suspicious look, which he countered with a bland expression. He knew she would not refuse, she thought ruefully. She smiled at Rosa and spoke whilst signing—*'I'll go and put my swimsuit on.'*

Stepping out of the changing cubicle a few minutes later, Darcey told herself it was ridiculous to feel self-conscious. Her yellow bikini was perfectly respectable. But she was supremely aware of Salvatore's intent gaze as she walked down the pool steps, and she quickly ducked under the water and swam away from him. She concentrated on Rosa, but although she did her best to ignore Salvatore she found her eyes straying to him, and her heart gave a jolt when she discovered he was watching her. Sexual tension simmered between them, fuelled by every furtive glance and the accidental contact of their bodies as they played in the pool with Rosa.

Darcey was relieved when Nico arrived, accompanied by the English nanny that Sergio and Kristen had hired to help with their growing family. Margaret was able to use sign language, and Salvatore had arranged for her to share her time between caring for Nico and Rosa.

'Nico has already been swimming in the pool at Casa Camelia,' Margaret explained. 'I'll take the children to play in the sandpit.'

Left alone with Salvatore, after Rosa had run off to play with her cousin, Darcey wrapped a towel around her shoulders, intending to go and change back into her clothes. But his deep voice stopped her.

'Surely you can take a break from working on your laptop and enjoy the sunshine?' His dark eyes gleamed with unexpected warmth. 'I already feel bad that you have missed your holiday in France.' Seeing Darcey hesitate, he added, 'While Margaret is taking care of the children I'd like you to give me an update on Rosa's progress.'

She could hardly refuse, but Darcey ignored the sun-lounger he had pulled up for her and went to sit beneath a parasol. 'I'll burn if I sit in the sun for more than a minute,' she told him. 'My mother has had a recent scare with a malignant melanoma so, much as I'd love a tan, I'm better off staying in the shade.'

'That's wise, with your fair skin, but you can be affected by UV rays even in the shade and it would be a good idea to use sunscreen.' Salvatore picked up the bottle of lotion, but instead of handing it to Darcey he tipped a blob of cream onto his palm and walked behind her.

She gasped at the feel of the cool lotion on her warm skin, but what made her heart beat even faster was the sensation of Salvatore's hands massaging her shoulders. Her body reacted instantly, and she was mortified when she looked down and saw the hard points of her nipples jutting beneath her bikini top.

'This is not appropriate,' she choked.

He bent his head and his soft laughter tickled her ear. 'Maybe not, but it's enjoyable—for both of us. Relax, *cara*, you're very tense.'

What did he expect? His touch was intensely sensual, and she could feel herself beginning to melt as desire pooled between her thighs.

'You wanted to discuss Rosa,' she reminded him desperately. 'Her confidence is growing daily, and it is vital that you continue to attend the speech therapy sessions to encourage her.' Darcey hesitated, wondering how she could help Salvatore to connect emotionally with his daughter. 'You are the most important person in Rosa's life,' she told him softly. 'She adores you.'

He abruptly snatched his hands from her shoulders. 'I wonder if she will when she discovers that it is my fault she does not have a mother.'

Knowing by now that he hated revealing his emotions,

Darcey expected him to walk away, but after a moment he pulled out a chair and sat down next to her beneath the parasol.

'Have you any idea what it feels like to know that I robbed my daughter of her mother?' he said harshly. 'Sometimes I've even wondered—' He broke off and swallowed hard.

Shocked by the pain she glimpsed in his eyes, Darcey said gently, 'You've wondered what?'

'Whether it is my fault she is deaf. I know that the medical reason was an ear infection, but perhaps the trauma of suddenly being separated from her mother contributed to Rosa's deafness.'

Darcey's heart ached for him, and she reached out and put her hand on his arm.

'I've read Rosa's medical notes. The most probable reason for her deafness is that during her birth excess fluid was trapped in the cochlea and damaged the tiny hair cells inside. It's called sensorineural hearing loss. It is possible that Rosa had moderate cochlear damage at birth and then a severe infection when she was a year old caused further damage and left her profoundly deaf, but I can assure you that the death of her mother, although traumatic, could not have caused Rosa to lose her hearing. You are not to blame, Salvatore,' she told him urgently. 'I don't know why or how the car accident happened, but I'm convinced that you would not have acted in a way that put Adriana's life at risk.'

He shook his head. 'What puzzles me most is that we were thrown out of the car, which means that we couldn't have been wearing seat belts. But I *always* wear a belt. I keep asking myself why I didn't wear one that night and insist that Adriana put a seat belt on?—especially when I was driving with the roof open.'

Salvatore closed his eyes as a searing pain shot through his head. Snatches of memory suddenly came into his mind.

He could see the sharp bend in the road ahead. He could feel the wind rushing through his hair. The car was travelling too fast. Fear churned in his stomach. He must turn the wheel and steer the car away from the edge of the road. But his hands were not on the wheel. He wasn't in control—and now it was too late...

'Salvatore?' Darcey's voice jerked him back to the present. 'What's wrong? Do you have a migraine?'

'No...' He raked a hand through his hair. 'Nothing is wrong.'

He was tempted to tell her about the images in his head, but what he had seen did not make sense. *Why* hadn't he been in control of the car just before it crashed?

He stared into Darcey's green eyes and felt a gentle tug on his heart. 'Thank you for putting my mind at rest about the cause of Rosa's deafness. I've always felt guilty,' he admitted roughly. 'A father is supposed to protect his child, but I believed I had caused her harm.'

Darcey's breath hitched in her throat as he lowered his head towards her. The atmosphere had altered subtly and sexual awareness throbbed between them as he brushed his mouth over hers. The kiss was frustratingly brief, but its sweetness pierced her heart and its promise of sensual ecstasy made her tremble.

'Rosa is coming,' he warned softly.

Darcey saw the regret she felt herself that he could not kiss her properly reflected in his eyes. Dragging oxygen into her lungs, she reached for her sunglasses to hide the devastating effect he had on her equilibrium.

Rosa dashed up to her father but then hesitated, as if she was unsure of her reception. Her wariness evoked a shaft of pain inside Salvatore. He had been so weighted down with his feelings of guilt that he had unwittingly pushed Rosa away, he realised heavily. Darcey had shown him that his little girl needed him and loved him. It was down to him to show Rosa that she meant the world to him.

Smiling, he opened his arms to her. For a second she looked surprised, but then she stepped into the circle of his arms and he hugged her tight.

Would you like to come to the stables with me? he signed. He was glad for once that he did not need to speak, because his throat burned with unfamiliar tears that he swallowed hastily as Rosa nodded eagerly. Salvatore glanced at Darcey and knew from the softness in her eyes that she had guessed his emotions were choking him.

'I'll spend some time with Rosa and meet you back at the castle later. Remember I'm hosting a business dinner party tonight? You'll join me, of course,' he said, forestalling the argument he could see she was about to make.

Without giving her a chance to reply he lifted his daughter onto his shoulders and strode away.

The path between the pool area and the castle ran beside the cliff-edge and provided wonderful views of the private bay belonging to the Castellano Estate. The colour of the sea reflected the azure blue of the sky, Darcey noted, and the pretty pink wildflowers growing along the edge of the path made a stunning contrast.

The late-afternoon sunshine felt hot on her shoulders and she was glad of the protection of her wide-brimmed hat. She was falling in love with Sicily, she thought, trying to ignore the voice inside her head which taunted that it was not only Sicily that had captured her heart.

With her mind on Salvatore, she took scant notice of the man who had stepped onto the path a little way ahead of her. She guessed he had walked up from the beach. She was used to seeing estate workers walking around the vast Castellano property, and would not have thought any more of it if the man hadn't looked over his shoulder. He was clearly startled when he saw her, and immediately turned back down the path leading to the beach. Darcey watched his rapidly retreating figure, feeling puzzled. She recognised him as the man she had seen arguing with Lydia in Taormina. But if Ettore Varsi worked on the Castellano estate surely Salvatore would have said so?

She was still wondering about the man on the path when she reached the castle. But as she entered the cool flagstoned hallway her thoughts turned to the dinner party tonight. Salvatore had said it was a business dinner for several wine importers from Eastern Europe whom he hoped to persuade to sell Castellano wine. It sounded a formal affair, and Darcey wondered what she should wear. Certainly the white cotton sundress she was wearing at the moment would not do.

She would ask Armond's advice, she decided. She had struck up a firm friendship with the butler, who seemed to belong at Torre d'Aquila as much as Salvatore did.

Armond could often be found in the dining room, but when Darcey walked into the room she was surprised to see Lydia, standing by the cabinet where the silverware was kept.

'*Oh*—I thought everyone was out,' Lydia said sharply. She seemed flustered. Especially when Darcey glanced at a silver snuff box sticking out of the large bag on the floor. 'I was just packing up some of the silverware to take it to be professionally polished,' she explained. 'My daughter liked everything in the castle to be properly cared for, and now that she is no longer here I have arranged with Salvatore that I will take on the responsibility of maintaining the castle's valuable antiques. Adriana loved the castle as much as Salvatore does.'

Yet Salvatore's only memory of his wife was that she had disliked living at Torre d'Aquila. Darcey did not say so to Lydia. 'I was looking for Armond,' she murmured.

'It's his afternoon off.' Lydia pushed the snuff box into the bag and closed the zip. 'He won't be back until dinner this evening.'

Just before eight o'clock Darcey entered the salon where she knew that cocktails would be served before dinner. None of the guests had yet arrived, and she hoped that if Salvatore thought her dress was unsuitable she would have time to run back upstairs and change.

He was standing by the bar, an imposing figure in a black tuxedo and so unfairly sexy that Darcey felt her stomach swoop. She noticed that he was clean-shaven for once. Without his customary black stubble shading his jaw he looked less like a pirate and more like a billionaire business tycoon.

He watched her walk into the room and his silence was telling.

'My dress is over the top, isn't it?' she said ruefully. 'I wasn't sure how formal the dinner party would be but I couldn't resist wearing the evening dress I bought to take to France.' She headed for the door. 'I'll go and put something else on.'

'Don't you dare!' Salvatore growled. He strode across the room with surprising speed, considering his injured leg, and stood in front of the door, blocking her path. 'You look beautiful.'

He studied her slender figure in the floor-length lilac

silk dress that skimmed her soft curves. The dress was strapless, showing off her bare shoulders and the upper slopes of her breasts. Her creamy skin was as smooth as fine porcelain, and closer inspection revealed a scattering of tiny golden freckles which matched the colour of the sun-lightened hair that framed her face.

He slowly shook his head. 'You always look beautiful. But tonight you are breathtaking, *mia bella*. Your dress is perfect.' He trapped her gaze and Darcey's heart beat a frantic tattoo when she saw molten desire in his eyes. '*You* are perfect, sweet Darcey, and I am going to spend the entire dinner fantasising about the gorgeous body beneath your dress.'

She blushed and wished she could make some witty, flirtatious response, but she felt tongue-tied and incredibly vulnerable, wondering if he was simply amusing himself with her. 'I wish you wouldn't tease me,' she mumbled.

'*Santa Madre!* You think I am teasing?' His voice deepened. 'I have never been more serious in my life, nor wanted any woman as urgently as I want you.' Salvatore's jaw clenched when he glimpsed the uncertainty in her eyes. 'I'd like to meet your ex-husband and let him know what I think of him for hurting you so badly,' he said harshly.

Darcey bit her lip. 'I was a fool to trust Marcus. Maybe I would be foolish to trust you too,' she said huskily. 'Lydia says you will never love another woman after Adriana, and that the women you have affairs with mean nothing to you. I...I don't think I could be happy to sleep with you knowing that in your eyes I am nothing.'

Her words grated on Salvatore's conscience. It was true that the few affairs he'd had since he had been widowed had been conducted almost exclusively in the bedroom. Sex without strings was fine when both parties agreed to it, and he had made sure his mistresses had been under no illusion that he might want a more meaningful relationship, but he had always known that Darcey was different from the women he'd had those casual affairs with.

'It is not true that you mean nothing to me,' he said harshly. 'I respect and admire you.'

The sentiments sounded hollow even to his own ears. Frustration surged through him as he fought the urge to pull Darcey into his arms and show her how goddamned good sex without the complication of emotions could be.

He jerked his eyes from her face as the salon door opened and Armond appeared to inform him that the guests had arrived.

Salvatore hated parties at the best of times, and tonight he wished he could send his guests away. But, if his father had done nothing else, Tito had at least drilled a sense of duty and a strong work ethic into him. Stifling his irritation, he instructed the butler to usher the guests in.

'We will continue this conversation later,' he told Darcey gruffly.

Her pink-glossed mouth was an irresistible temptation, and with an oath he slanted his lips over hers in a brief, unsatisfactory kiss that left him aching for more.

CHAPTER EIGHT

DARCEY WAS FORCED to call on all her acting skills to appear calm and collected as Salvatore introduced her to his dinner guests. He gave no explanation of her role at the castle, and she was sure his business associates assumed she was his mistress—especially when he slipped his arm possessively around her waist as they walked through to the dining room.

Lydia was late, as usual, and as they took their places at the table Armond informed Salvatore that she would not be joining them at all because she was feeling unwell. Thinking of Salvatore's mother-in-law reminded Darcey of the man she had seen when she had walked back from the pool: the same man who had been arguing with Lydia in Taormina a few days ago.

'Did Ettore Varsi come to visit Lydia?' she asked. 'I saw him earlier today, on the path by the beach.'

Salvatore frowned. 'I was not informed by the security guards that Ettore had visited the estate. Perhaps you mistook one of the workers for him?'

'No, it was definitely him.' Darcey was absolutely certain it *had* been Ettore she had seen, and felt irritated that Salvatore clearly did not believe her.

The conversation around the dinner table quickly turned to business, but Darcey did not mind. She was preoccupied with her thoughts. Salvatore made an effort to be a charming host, but she sensed his impatience with social niceties and knew he would rather be at the winery or out in the vineyards than making polite small talk. He was a man of action rather than words, and she had a feeling that the same would be true in the bedroom.

Thinking about making love with him brought a flush to her cheeks, and her colour deepened when she felt his brooding gaze on her. Did she dare respond to the glittering desire in his eyes? Why shouldn't she enjoy a brief fling with him? She smiled ruefully to herself when she remembered her mother's advice to have a sizzling affair with a sexy Sicilian. She had told her mother that Salvatore was dangerous, and now she knew it to be true. He was a serious threat to her heart, and for that reason she was hesitant about them becoming lovers.

It was late when the guests departed. Darcey stood with Salvatore on the steps of the castle and watched the tail-lights of the cars disappear down the driveway. There was no moon or stars tonight, and the darkness closed around them like an impenetrable cloak.

'A storm is brewing,' he predicted. 'Can you feel the electricity in the air?'

Something was certainly making the hairs on the back of her neck prickle, but she had a feeling it was the smouldering sensuality of the man beside her rather than the atmospheric conditions. Darcey's heart-rate accelerated as Salvatore slipped his arm around her waist and led her back into the castle. An unspoken question hovered between them, but she was no closer to the answer than she had been during dinner. Her body ached with longing for him to take her to bed, but the voice of caution inside her head was determined not to be ignored.

Salvatore lifted his hand and tucked a few silky strands of copper-brown hair behind Darcey's ear.

'Sweet Darcey, what am I going to do about you?' he murmured, half beneath his breath.

He was on fire for her and the throb of his arousal could only be assuaged by making love to her. If she had been any other woman he would have whisked her off to bed long ago, but the indecision in her green eyes stalled him and the faint tremor of her mouth tugged on his conscience.

The sound of brisk footsteps on the stone floor shattered the tense silence. Salvatore frowned as he glanced towards the butler, who had appeared in the doorway.

'You may retire for the night, Armond. I will turn off the lights when I go to bed.'

'I must speak to you about an urgent matter, *signore*.' The butler was clearly troubled. 'Some items of silverware are missing from the cabinet in the dining room. I only noticed when I replaced the cutlery after dinner and saw that some pieces at the back of the cabinet were out of place. When I looked I realised several valuable antiques have disappeared. The items concerned are not used regularly and I cannot say when they went missing,' he added regretfully.

Armond looked deeply upset. Darcey knew he took great pride in his duties at the castle and she quickly reassured him. 'It's all right, Armond. Lydia—Signora Putzi—took some of the silver ornaments away to be professionally polished. I saw her take them out of the cabinet this afternoon. I assumed you knew,' she said slowly, when the butler looked puzzled.

'I assure you that I take excellent care of the silverware and polish all the pieces regularly,' Armond said in an affronted voice.

'No doubt there is an explanation,' Salvatore murmured. 'Armond, will you go and ask Signora Putzi to come down to my study? She is forever telling me that she has trouble sleeping, so she is probably still awake,' he told Darcey drily.

Ten minutes later Armond ushered an irate Lydia into the study. 'What on earth is going on?' she demanded. 'Why have you disturbed me at this time of night?'

Her anger turned to outrage when Salvatore briefly explained about the missing silver and she shot Darcey a furious look.

'Of *course* I didn't take anything out of the cabinet. I've never heard such nonsense. Darcey is obviously lying and trying to put the blame for the disappearance of the silver on to me, when in actual fact *she* must have taken the items.'

'But…I saw you in the dining room earlier, taking things from the cabinet,' Darcey faltered, stunned by Lydia's denial. 'You told me —'

'I was in my room all afternoon, reading,' Lydia snapped.

'Did you meet up with Ettore Varsi? I saw him in the grounds of the estate this afternoon, and I saw you talking to him in Taormina the other day.'

For a moment Lydia looked startled, but she quickly recovered and turned to face Salvatore. 'I have no idea what Darcey is talking about. I haven't seen Ettore for months. I'm going back to bed,' she said regally. She flicked a scathing glance at Darcey. 'I understand your game, Miss Rivers. You've set your sights on Salvatore and you want me out of the way because I am a reminder of the love he had for my daughter. Don't bother to deny it. I've seen the way you look at my son-in-law. But you are not the first stupid girl to have a crush on him and I don't suppose you will be the last. Just don't fool your-self into thinking that you will ever be more than a con-venient outlet for his physical needs—'

'*That's enough!*' Salvatore interrupted the older woman sharply. 'You know nothing about my relation-ship with Darcey.'

'I'm simply telling her the truth.' Lydia glared at him, but then her face crumpled. 'I adored my Adriana but she was stolen from me. You were responsible for her death, Salvatore, and the least you can do is to remain faithful to her memory.'

Lydia swept out of the room, and in the ensuing silence her ugly accusations seemed to echo around the study.

'I *did* see her take the silverware from the cabinet,' Darcey insisted. 'I don't understand why she denied it.' Nor did she understand why Lydia had denied speaking to Ettore Varsi in Taormina. She glanced at Salvatore, but his hard features revealed nothing of his thoughts. 'You do believe me…don't you?'

His reply did nothing to reassure her. 'I'm sure there is a reasonable explanation for everything,' he said curtly. 'I suggest you go to bed and we will discuss the situa-tion in the morning.'

Salvatore stared at Darcey's hurt expression and felt a surge of frustration. His instincts told him she was speaking the truth about the missing silver, yet it made no sense. Why would Lydia take the things? And why did Darcey insist that she had seen Ettore Varsi?

'The man you saw today cannot have been Ettore. The only access to the estate is through the main gates, which are guarded around the clock. I asked the secu-rity guards to check through the CCTV footage, in case they had forgotten about his visit, but his car doesn't ap-pear on the film.'

'Do you think I'm lying?' she demanded hotly.

Salvatore shook his head. 'I think you were mistaken.'

Which was as good as saying he thought she was lying, Darcey thought grimly as she marched out of the study. Too much was going on that she did not understand, and Lydia's inexplicable behaviour tonight further fuelled the mystery. As she ran upstairs to her bedroom she recalled Lydia's accusation that she had a crush on Salvatore and her face burned with mortification. Had she really been so obvious? Maybe Salvatore had believed she would fall into his bed with little persuasion. But now he thought she was a liar and a thief and that was why he had looked at her with cold disdain.

Angry tears stung her eyes. Things would have been so much easier if he had never strolled into her office in London and turned her life upside down. She wished she had not come to Sicily, but deep in her heart she wished even more that she was not destined to leave Torre d'Aquila at the end of the summer. The painful truth was that she had fallen fathoms deep in love with Salvatore, but his heart was buried with his dead wife.

The storm broke over the castle with a lightning flare outside the window that briefly lit up the bedroom before it died away to leave the room in complete darkness. A giant thunderclap shook the ancient walls and Darcey jerked awake. She fumbled to switch on the bedside lamp and realised that the castle must have suffered a power cut.

Remembering the candles on the chest of drawers, she slid off the bed, grimacing at the thought that her dress was probably creased because she had fallen asleep fully clothed. Lightning flared again, and the ensuing darkness was so black that for a moment she felt disorientated. She immediately thought of Rosa. The little girl would not be disturbed by the thunder, because her cochlear implant device was switched off, but if the lightning woke her she would be terrified of the dark and would not understand why the nightlight in her room did not work.

Another flare of lightning enabled Darcey to locate and light a candle, but as she hurried down the corridor the feeble light it emitted threatened to sputter out. At least she could reassure the child if she woke up, she thought. But as she pushed open Rosa's bedroom door she bumped into something big and solid and could not restrain a squeak of surprise.

Salvatore was holding an old-fashioned oil lamp, and the flame cast flickering shadows on the walls and over the chiselled contours of his face.

'I should have known that your first concern would be Rosa,' he said in a curious tone. 'As you have no doubt realised, the power is out. Unfortunately the castle does not have a backup generator, but the oil lamps are always kept filled. I've lit one in Rosa's room and it should last until morning.' He glanced at the dim light from Darcey's candle and blew across the flame gently to extinguish it. 'I'd better come and light a lamp in your room.'

He led her back along the corridor and ushered her into her room, holding the lamp high to guide her. As the lamplight flickered across her face Salvatore frowned.

'Why have you been crying? It's pointless to deny it—your eyes look like shimmering green pools,' he said roughly.

'What did you expect after I've been unjustly accused of being a thief?' Darcey's voice trembled. 'You made it plain that you believe Lydia rather than me.'

Recalling his cold expression down in the study, she gave a choked cry and whirled around, wanting to get away from him. He was still blocking her path to the door, and with no clear thought in her head as to what she was doing she ran across to the French doors leading to the balcony.

The storm was in full fury and the rain was falling so hard that it lashed her bare arms when she stepped outside. Darcey's emotions were in tatters. The scene in Salvatore's study, when his silence had implied that he thought she had stolen the silverware, had left her feeling as hurt and humiliated as she had been when she had walked in on Marcus having sex with his mistress.

She lifted her face to the sky, so that the rain disguised her tears, but Salvatore had followed her onto the balcony and he caught hold of her shoulder and spun her round to him.

'I never thought for a second that you took the silver,' he said fiercely. 'I don't know why Lydia lied, but I've no doubt the truth will be revealed. I certainly do not doubt your honesty. How could I, when I have witnessed every day since I brought you to Torre d'Aquila your sweet nature, your kindness and your abundant compassion?'

His voice deepened, caressing Darcey's senses and soothing her hurt pride.

'I would trust you with my life, *mia bella*.'

His dark eyes blazed, as if he was determined to make her believe him. He cupped her cheek, and to Darcey's amazement his hand was unsteady.

'You accuse me of regarding you as unimportant, but that is not true.' His mouth twisted. 'My amnesia makes me feel that I am trapped in a dark tunnel with no beginning or end. The truth is that I don't know *what* I feel, but I am certain that I have never felt this way about any other woman. It's not just sexual attraction,' he insisted as she opened her mouth to speak. 'For most of my life after my mother abandoned me I put up barriers and pushed people away. Even my twin brother and my own daughter could not thaw the coldness inside me. But I don't want to push *you* away, *carissima*.'

He threaded his other hand through her hair and lowered his head so that Darcey could feel his warm breath on her rain-soaked face.

'I want to hold you close and make love to you. I want to show you how perfect it will be for us.'

How could she deny him when she wanted him with all her heart? Darcey thought. Salvatore had made no promises. He had admitted honestly that he did not know how he felt. But the fact that he felt *something*, and had opened up his emotions as much as he had, allayed her doubts. She understood that his difficult upbringing meant he found it hard to give his trust, and she was deeply moved by his avowal that he would trust her with his life.

'I want to make love with you too,' she told him huskily.

The confession brought a sense of release, as if she had been set free from the past. She was no longer the naive girl she had been during her marriage. Salvatore had restored the self-confidence that her ex-husband had destroyed and she wasn't ashamed to admit that she desired him. But she would come to him as his equal, she vowed. She was not a timid virgin.

Lifting her hands to his face, she urged his mouth down on hers.

It was like putting a match to dry tinder. The first touch of his lips on hers set their passion alight, as if all the weeks of sexual frustration, the secretive glances and sleepless nights tormented by longing, were bound up in the kiss. Darcey parted her lips as Salvatore deepened the kiss until she was aware of nothing but him, the slight roughness of his jaw against her cheek and the sheer eroticism of his tongue pushing into her mouth. She knew there would be no turning back now. Soon she and Salvatore would be lovers.

The prospect caused her heart to skitter with a mixture of nervous excitement and anticipation, and when he wrapped his arms around her and crushed her against his broad chest she melted into his embrace.

He had known Darcey was trouble the minute he'd walked into her office, Salvatore thought. His instincts had told him that beneath her prim suit she was a sensual, exciting—he glanced up at the torrential rain falling from the heavens and gave a wry smile—and unpredictable woman.

'You're soaked through,' he growled, running his hands over her sodden dress, which was sticking to her body like a second skin.

'So are you.'

With a boldness he had not expected she tugged open the buttons of his shirt and parted the wet material to skim her hands over his naked chest. Desire corkscrewed through him when she flicked her tongue over one of his nipples, and without another word he lifted her into his arms and carried her back into the bedroom.

The light from the oil lamp cast a gentle glow over the room and softened Salvatore's hard features a little. The first time she had seen him he had reminded her of a medieval knight, Darcey remembered. But at that first meeting his eyes had been cold and expressionless, whereas now they were lit with a sultry heat that set her heart pounding.

'You're shivering,' he said softly. 'Are you cold?'

She met his gaze and Salvatore noticed that her eyes had darkened to jade.

'No, I'm not cold.'

Another tremor ran through her, and he understood. The same urgent desire was making his body shake.

'You need to get out of your wet dress,' he murmured. Stepping behind her, he ran the zip down her spine.

Darcey caught her breath when the strapless silk bodice slithered down. Her eyes were drawn to the floor-length mirror on the wall opposite them as Salvatore slid his arms around her and cupped her bare breasts in his hands. The contrast of his tanned fingers with her pale flesh was incredibly erotic. He towered above her, this dark, enigmatic man, master of Torre d'Aquila, keeper of her heart.

Her pulse quickened as she watched their reflection, watched him stroke his thumb-pads across her nipples and then roll them between his fingers until they swelled to hard points. The pleasure was so intense that she gave a little moan and tried to turn to face him, but he tightened his arms around her so that she was trapped against him.

'Do you like that, *mia bella*?' he whispered in her ear.

When she nodded he squeezed her nipples harder, seeming to know instinctively the fine line between pleasure and pain.

Liquid heat pooled between Darcey's thighs when she felt the hard ridge of his arousal push against the cleft of her bottom. She was desperate for him to touch her intimately, and he must have sensed her impatience for he gripped her dress and tugged it down over her hips so that it fell to the floor, leaving her in just a pair of lilac lace knickers. Darcey's mouth ran dry as she watched in the mirror as Salvatore skimmed his hand down over her flat stomach to the edge of her panties. She swallowed when he eased his fingers beneath the fragile barrier of silk and stroked the tight cluster of copper-coloured curls that hid her femininity.

Mesmerised by the erotic image reflected in the mirror, she widened her eyes as she felt him part her and slide his finger inside her. He gave a feral groan as he discovered the slick heat of her arousal. His eyes met hers in the mirror as he began to caress her, and almost instantly she felt her body tighten.

'Salvatore…' She breathed his name, warning him that she was close to orgasm. She did not want him to stop what he was doing with his fingers, but he had aroused a greater need in her that only his full possession could satisfy.

Finally he allowed her to turn around, and immediately lowered his head to take first one dusky nipple and then the other into his mouth. Darcey gasped with the exquisite sensations he was arousing. With feverish haste she pushed his shirt over his shoulders so that she could run her hands over his naked chest. Boldly she moved lower and unfastened his belt buckle.

'Don't stop, *carissima*,' Salvatore bade her roughly when she hesitated.

She stared at his face, all angles and planes in the flickering lamplight, and her stomach clenched when she saw the primitive desire in his eyes. Returning to her task, she freed his zip and pushed his trousers over his hips, realising that he was barefoot. He stepped out of his trousers with easy grace, but instead of touching her he waited, his expression hidden beneath heavy eyelids, while her gaze moved to the mass of deep scars on his thigh. Darcey had seen them before in the pool, but up close the purple welts were a shocking reminder of the terrible injuries he had sustained in the car accident.

Gently she ran her fingerers over the scars and felt him flinch.

'I'm sorry. I didn't mean to hurt you,' she whispered.

'You didn't,' he assured her. 'But if you carry on touching me I hope you are prepared for the consequences.'

'If I touch you like this, do you mean?' she asked innocently, slipping her hand beneath the hem of one leg of his boxer shorts and lightly stroking his swollen penis.

'Madonna!' Salvatore's restraint shattered and he dragged her against him, capturing her mouth in a fiercely possessive kiss. With a deft movement he pulled off his boxers and stood before her, proudly naked and magnificently aroused.

Darcey drew a startled breath when she saw the size of him, but her faint trepidation was forgotten when he slanted his lips over hers and kissed her with sensual passion. The room tilted as he lifted her into his arms and laid her on the bed.

The hard glitter in his eyes told her the time for teasing and foreplay was over. A shadow of her old self-doubt returned when he pulled her panties off and ran his eyes slowly over her naked body. She thought of the photographs she had seen of his gorgeous wife. Adriana had possessed a voluptuous figure. Did Salvatore wish that her breasts were fuller and her hips more rounded? Darcey wondered.

He stroked his hand lightly over her stomach and gave a hoarse groan as he caressed the soft skin of her inner thighs. 'You take my breath away, *mia bella*. The instant I met you I imagined making love to you, and now I can't wait any longer.'

She shared his impatience and offered no resistance when he pushed her legs apart. It was new to her, this uncontrollable hunger that consumed her, and it was a little frightening to find herself at the mercy of her need for sexual fulfilment. But she was enslaved by her need for Salvatore, and when he lifted himself above her she arched her hips, trembling, eager, as the tip of his manhood pressed against her core. As he eased forward she opened for him, catching her breath when her internal muscles had to stretch to accommodate him.

He stilled and stared into her eyes. 'Are you all right? I don't want to hurt you.'

'I'm fine,' she assured him. This pirate was as dangerous as she had guessed him to be, but his tenderness was unexpected.

He kissed her again, gently at first, and she felt a pull on her emotions. But as he deepened the kiss she stopped thinking and gave herself up to the firestorm of passion building inside her as he penetrated her fully and filled her with his swollen length.

Salvatore withdrew and then drove into her again, slowly at first, increasing Darcey's excitement with each measured stroke. It felt so unbelievably good, and she sensed from his quickened breathing that his pleasure was as intense as hers. His dark hair fell forward and she brushed it back from his face before tracing the shape of his chiselled features with shaking fingers. Some deeply primitive instinct insisted that this was her man. The moment she'd met him she'd had a strange sense that she belonged to him, and now, as he thrust into her again and again, she felt that they were joined body and soul.

It couldn't last. Their mutual hunger was too intense. Darcey tensed as she felt ripples of sensation begin deep in her pelvis, and she clung to Salvatore's sweat-sheened shoulders as he quickened his pace. She gasped as he slid his hands beneath her bottom and angled her to take an even deeper thrust. She should have guessed that to be possessed by a pirate would be more compelling, more intense than anything she had ever experienced, she thought. But then her mind went blank and sensation took over. Her climax was hard and fast—pulse-waves of pleasure throbbing through her body. At the same time she heard Salvatore make a harsh sound as his orgasm overpowered him.

For a long time afterwards they remained still joined, breathing hard. In the aftermath of the most passionate lovemaking Salvatore had ever known he felt a sense of contentment that he had never experienced before. For the first time in his life he felt truly relaxed and at peace.

He watched Darcey's copper-gold eyelashes drift closed. Her creamy skin was flushed rose-pink, both on her face and her breasts, he noted, feeling a swift resurgence of desire. He resisted the urge to wake her and take her again. He'd guessed from the slight resistance of her internal muscles when he had initially thrust into her that she had not had sex for a while, and he told himself to be patient. She had agreed to stay at the castle until the end of summer. There would be plenty of opportunities to make love to her. It occurred to him that maybe he could persuade her to extend her stay, and that thought was followed by the realisation that he was in no hurry for her to leave.

Lying back on the pillows, he turned his mind to his niggling concerns about the missing silver antiques and his mother-in-law's curious behaviour. He did not doubt that Darcey had seen Lydia take the silver from the cabinet, but if there was a simple explanation why had Lydia reacted so strangely?

There was also the question of Ettore Varsi. Again, Salvatore believed Darcey. There was no reason why she would have made up the story that she had seen Ettore on the Castellano Estate. But why had he been here? And why had he been careful to avoid the security guards?

Ettore had been on his mind a lot recently. After the accident Salvatore had been grateful to the man who had saved his life by dragging him away from the car before it burst into flames. He had given Ettore a significant financial reward. But for reasons he could not explain to himself he had never liked the man. When Darcey had tried to persuade him to talk to Ettore about the accident, in the hope that something would kick-start his memory, he had shot her down, convinced that there could be no absolution for him. He had been driving the car and he must have been responsible for the crash. But in his last few flashbacks, his wisps of memory were frustratingly incomplete, and if they were true they did not make sense.

Salvatore closed his eyes, hoping that the dull throb behind his temples that had begun a few minutes ago would lessen. But the pain intensified until his head felt as though it would explode. He was almost tempted to wake Darcey and seek solace in the gentle compassion he knew she would offer. He pushed the thought away. He had never asked anyone for help in his life and he wasn't about to start now. Instead he gritted his teeth and waited for the headache to pass. The oil lamp had gone out, and as he stared into the darkness the shadows that had clouded his mind for so long shifted.

Darcey opened her eyes to find her bedroom was filled with bright sunlight. For a moment she wondered if she had dreamed the storm of the previous night. The rumpled sheets and the slight soreness between her legs warned her that she had not imagined making love with Salvatore. He had spent the night in her bed, or at least part of the night. She had no idea when he had left her room—or why he had chosen not to stay with her. Did he regret what had happened? She bit her lip as her old insecurities surfaced. Perhaps he regretted betraying the memory of his wife?

She was distracted from her thoughts when Rosa skipped into the bedroom, carrying a pile of storybooks. Salvatore was aware that Rosa came to her room most mornings, and it was understandable that he would not have wanted his daughter to discover him in bed with her, Darcey's common sense pointed out.

'I'd better get up,' she said, and signed to the little girl. 'I'll read to you after breakfast.'

Darcey took a quick shower and dressed in a white cotton skirt and a green strap top, pleased to see that her usually pale skin had gained a light golden tan during the time she had been in Sicily. It only took a couple of minutes to dry her hair, and with no other excuse to avoid meeting Salvatore she went to find Rosa and take her down to the dining room for breakfast.

The English nanny, Margaret, was in the nursery. 'I think it might be a good idea if I take Rosa to Casa Camelia to play with Nico,' the nanny said. 'There seems to be an argument going on downstairs between Signora Putzi and Signore Castellano. It's probably best if Rosa is kept away from the situation. Things sound rather heated.'

Puzzled by what Margaret had said, Darcey realised she could hear raised voices when she went downstairs. She hesitated when she saw Salvatore and Lydia in the entrance hall and felt a jolt of shock as she recognised the man with them as Ettore Varsi—whom Lydia had sworn she had not seen for months.

Wearing black jeans, shirt and riding boots, and with a grim expression on his face, Salvatore looked formidable as he faced Lydia. 'Explain why you took the silver antiques,' he demanded.

'So you believe the word of that little tart?' Lydia snapped. 'You fool, Salvatore. It's obvious that Darcey is hoping to snare a rich lover and she doesn't want me around to interfere with her plans.'

'Leave Darcey out of this,' he said in a dangerously soft voice. 'Of course I believe her. She is the most honest and honourable person I have ever met. But the same cannot be said of *you*, Lydia. You were caught on the security cameras leaving the castle early this morning, carrying the bag Darcey described, which she had seen you filling with silverware. At the same time Ettore was caught by my security guards landing his boat on the Castellano Estate's private beach.'

Suddenly sensing Darcey's presence, Salvatore glanced towards the stairs.

'I'll—I'll go,' she stammered, her heart sinking as she stared at his stern features. It was impossible to believe that he had made love to her with such tender passion last night.

'No, I want you to stay.'

He sought her gaze, and for a second she glimpsed a flare of emotion in his dark eyes that shook her.

He returned his attention to his mother-in-law and the man with her, who looked as if he would rather be somewhere else. 'I suspect you took the silver to give to Ettore,' Salvatore told Lydia. 'But I want you to tell me why.'

'This is ridiculous—treating me like a criminal,' Lydia blustered. 'I admit I…*borrowed*…some silverware, but I don't know why Ettore came to the Castellano Estate.'

'I was fishing,' Ettore muttered. 'I had trouble with

my boat and I was forced to land on the beach. I don't know—'

'*Enough!*' Salvatore's voice cracked like a whip and both Lydia and Ettore stared at him nervously. 'Before you tell me any more lies you need to know that I have regained my memory—and I remember *everything* about the accident.'

CHAPTER NINE

DARCEY'S SENSE OF shock was mirrored on Lydia's face. Salvatore's mother-in-law turned pale and covered her face with her hands. 'Oh, my God. I didn't think it could happen after all this time…'

Ettore Varsi had also paled. He spun round and ran across the hall to the front door, but was apprehended by two security guards waiting outside. Salvatore strode over to him and grabbed him by the lapels of his jacket.

'You lied, didn't you?' he said harshly. 'I *wasn't* driving the car when it crashed. Adriana was driving. For the past four years all I could remember was getting behind the steering wheel when we left the party. But now I remember that on the journey home I stopped. Adriana and I were having a row and I knew it wasn't safe to drive when I had lost my temper.'

He tightened his grip on Ettore.

'I remember seeing you drive past while we were standing at the side of the road arguing. Adriana suddenly jumped into the driver's seat of my car. She was drunk and I was scared for her safety. As she pulled away I managed to leap into the passenger seat. I was pleading with her to slow down when we overtook you on the road.'

Salvatore's voice roughened.

'I remember approaching the bend and knowing that we weren't going to make it. Adriana was going too fast. I tried to grab the wheel, but it was too late. The last memory I have is of the car smashing through the barrier and hurtling down the mountainside. *Why did you lie to the police?*' he asked Ettore savagely. 'Why did you allow me to believe that the accident was my fault?'

'She told me to do it.' Ettore pointed to Lydia.

He looked terrified, and when Darcey glanced at Salvatore's murderous expression she wasn't surprised.

'It was her idea.'

Salvatore flung Ettore away, as if he felt contaminated by the other man's presence. 'I don't believe you. It can't be true.' He looked at his mother-in-law and frowned as Lydia burst into tears.

'It *is* true,' she wept. 'There's no point pretending any more. I was staying here at the castle the night the accident happened, and as soon as I heard the news I rushed to the scene of the crash. I wanted to save my baby, but Adriana was already dead.'

She gave a tearing sob that wrenched Darcey's heart.

'I saw Ettore,' she continued. 'He was waiting to give a statement to the police. He told me what had happened—how he had seen Adriana driving erratically just before the crash.' She looked pleadingly at Salvatore. 'I guessed she would have got drunk at the party. She loved champagne. Adriana was a top model and you are a member of the renowned Castellano family, so I knew the crash would be headline news around the world. I couldn't bear the thought of my daughter being blamed for the accident and the media tearing her reputation to shreds. I loved my darling girl and I…I wanted to protect her name.'

Lydia took a shuddering breath.

'So I offered money to Ettore if he would give a false

statement to the police. He had pulled you and Adriana away from the car before it caught fire. There was no way of proving who had been driving—there was just Ettore's word.'

'*Santa Madre,*' Salvatore said raggedly. 'All this time you let me think I had killed Adriana and robbed Rosa of her mother. You *knew* I was tortured with guilt...'

'You didn't love Adriana,' Lydia said bitterly. 'You only married her because she was pregnant and you wanted the child. You deserved to suffer like I was suffering.' Taking another shuddering breath, she continued. 'At first everything worked out. I paid Ettore to keep quiet about what he knew. But he kept asking for more money and I couldn't meet his demands. I am not wealthy. My husband lost a fortune in a bad business deal and when he died I inherited very little. Luckily your guilt over Adriana meant that you allowed me to stay at the castle, which cut down my living expenses.'

'So that's why you kept telling me how much I had loved Adriana. You played on my conscience.'

The raw pain in Salvatore's voice was too much for Darcey to bear and she hurried over to him and gripped his hand. He did not look at her, but he squeezed her fingers in acknowledgement of her support.

'You must have prayed that I would never regain my memory,' he said grimly to Lydia.

'You were different when you came back from England.' She glanced at Darcey. 'It's not hard to guess why. I knew that if you had an affair with Darcey you might not want me around. I told Ettore I couldn't give him any more money, but he insisted. In desperation I agreed to take some of the silver antiques, so that he could sell them. There are so many valuable items in the castle I didn't think anyone would notice if a few went missing.'

'Armond has catalogued every item,' Darcey murmured.

She looked towards the front door as a commotion broke out. Ettore had managed to escape from the security guards and was tearing down the front steps of the castle.

'Let him go,' Salvatore advised the guards. 'He won't get far now that the security staff have moved his boat from the beach. He'll be arrested when I tell the police that he gave a false statement and has been involved in blackmail. I hope he rots in jail, and if I get hold of him he'll think he's in hell,' he said bitterly.

His expression turned to disgust as he studied Lydia, who was still crying. He was patently unmoved by her tears. 'I'll give you five minutes to pack and then I want you to leave my home for good.'

'But…surely you will allow me to visit my granddaughter occasionally?' Lydia whispered.

'After what you have done you're lucky I have decided not to press charges against you. But you will never be welcome at Torre d'Aquila again.'

Lydia gasped and her shoulders shook as more sobs tore through her. Darcey's soft heart ached for the older woman, despite all that she had done.

She put a comforting hand on Lydia's arm and stared at Salvatore, her green eyes bright with emotion. 'That's too cruel,' she said softly.

His jaw clenched. 'How can you defend her after she let me suffer for four hellish years?'

'I know what she did was terrible, but she has lost her only daughter. Rosa is her only link with Adriana.'

Darcey bit her lip as Salvatore's dark eyes burned into her. She knew he thought she was being disloyal by sympathising with Lydia. His mouth twisted and he growled something ugly before he swung away from her and strode out of the castle. She longed to run after him, but Lydia collapsed onto the floor and Darcey hurriedly called to Armond for help.

'I can't believe Lydia and Ettore did such a terrible thing,' Kristen said for about the tenth time. She shook her head. 'Lying to Salvatore and letting him think he was responsible for Adriana's death was unforgivable. No wonder he was so angry when he came and told Sergio this morning. But at least he has regained his memory at last.'

Darcey glanced across the charming sitting room at Casa Camelia, where she had spent the day. Kristen was picking up the toys that Nico and Rosa had been playing with before the nanny had taken them outside to the garden.

'I'm glad Salvatore confided in Sergio. When he left the castle after Lydia had confessed, he looked—' Darcey broke off, unable to explain Salvatore's savage expression or the flash of hurt in his eyes when she was sympathetic to Lydia.

Kristen nodded. 'It was tragic that the brothers were separated when they were young boys and didn't share the bond many twins have. But they are closer now. Salvatore has always seemed so self-contained, but recently I've noticed a change in him, and Sergio has mentioned it too.' She gave Darcey a speculative look. 'Salvatore seems more relaxed since you have been staying at the castle. What *is* going on between the two of you?'

Darcey felt heat rise in her face. 'Nothing,' she said quickly. 'At least nothing serious.' She bit her lip as she recalled their passionate lovemaking the previous night. For all she knew he might have regarded having sex with

her as a one-night stand. 'Salvatore doesn't allow anyone too close.'

'And yet I sense that he would like to get close to
you,' Kristen's bright blue eyes softened when she saw
that Darcey was uncomfortable with the conversation.
'I wonder when the men will be back. They went out on
the horses hours ago.' She focused on the tiny baby in
Darcey's arms. 'Talking of men—how is my little man?'

'He's still asleep.' Darcey looked down at baby Leo's
angelic face and felt a deep pull of maternal longing in
the pit of her stomach. 'He's gorgeous,' she murmured.

Kristen laughed. 'Like all the Castellano men.' She
glanced out of the window at her older son Nico, who
was racing across the patio with Rosa. 'I think our five
minutes of peace is about to end,' she said ruefully.

Darcey took Rosa back to the castle in the early evening. The little girl was tired after spending the day with
her energetic cousin, and fell asleep within minutes of
Darcey tucking her into bed. She had not seen or heard
from Salvatore all day, but a few minutes after she had
walked into her bedroom Armond knocked on the door.

'Signore Castellano has asked me to inform you that
dinner will be served in the tower room this evening.'
The butler handed her a large flat box. 'He also asked
me to give you this.'

Puzzled, she carried the box over to the bed and
gasped when she opened it and lifted out an exquisite
dress. The floor-length cream chiffon gown was beautifully understated and she recognised the logo on the box
as belonging to a top design house. The last time she had
seen Salvatore he had seemed bitterly angry with her.
She had no idea why he had given her the dress, or why

he had arranged for them to eat in her favourite room in the castle.

With an hour to spare before dinner she indulged in a pampering session, and after a long soak, fragrant with bath crystals, she smoothed scented oil onto her skin and dried her hair into a glossy bob before slipping the dress over her head. The low-cut neckline revealed the smooth upper slopes of her breasts and the narrow shoulder straps embellished with crystals added sparkle to the elegant gown.

Her heart was thudding by the time she reached the tower room, and although she told herself she was breathless because she had climbed four flights of stairs, the truth was that she felt nervous at the prospect of being alone with Salvatore for the first time since she had been naked in his arms.

She opened the door and stepped into the circular room, which had windows all the way round the walls, giving stunning vistas of the Sicilian countryside and the smouldering volcano Etna towering in the distance. But Darcey barely noticed the view. Her eyes were drawn to Salvatore.

Silhouetted against the evening sunshine streaming through the windows, his face was in shadow. She was aware of his exceptional height and the power of his formidable build. Wearing close-fitting black trousers and a fine white shirt, his dark hair brushing his shoulders, he would not have looked out of place in a previous century, she thought ruefully.

He studied her for long moments, while Darcey's tension grew, but then, to her amazement, his mouth curved into a warm smile that trapped her breath in her lungs.

'You look even more beautiful in the dress than I imagined when I chose it for you,' he murmured.

'It's the loveliest dress I've ever worn.' She swallowed. 'I...I thought you would still be angry with me.'

'Angry with *you*?' he sounded genuinely surprised. 'Why would you think that, *carissima*?'

'Because I asked you to show leniency to Lydia.'

Her heart missed a beat as Salvatore crossed the room and stood in front of her. He slid his hand beneath her chin and she felt a jolt of shock when she saw that the warmth of his smile was reflected in his eyes. The change in him was remarkable. His face was no longer set in a stern expression and there was a new softness to his chiselled features that made Darcey's insides melt.

'I knew even as I stormed out of the castle this morning that I should not have expected anything less from you. Your compassionate heart puts me to shame.'

'You have every right to be furious and bitter,' she said huskily. 'Lydia and Ettore did a terrible thing. Ettore lied purely for financial gain, and I hope he is sent to prison, but I can understand why Lydia wanted to protect her daughter even after her death. She loved Adriana so much.' Darcey hesitated. 'Lydia accused you of not loving Adriana. If that is true, why did you marry her?'

Salvatore exhaled heavily. 'I find it amazing that after four years of blankness I am suddenly able to remember everything about my past—including my relationship with Adriana. I met her in Rome. I was there on business and she was modelling at a charity fashion show that I was invited to.' He shrugged. 'I found her attractive and we became lovers. But to be honest I had no intention of prolonging our affair after I returned to Sicily. That was until three months later, when Adriana turned up at the castle and announced she was expecting my baby. A DNA test proved it *was* my child. She insisted that the condom must have been faulty, but I suspect she aimed to fall pregnant as a means of gaining financial security once she realised the extent of my wealth. It's not an unusual story, is it? Rich guy gets trapped by unscrupulous gold-digger,' he said sardonically. 'But I immediately accepted responsibility for my child and did the only thing I could do under the circumstances—married Adriana. It was certainly no love-match, but I was determined to try to make the marriage work for the sake of our child. And when Rosa was born I fell in love.

'Not with Adriana,' he said in answer to Darcey's questioning look. 'The moment I held my daughter in my arms I was overwhelmed by an emotion I had never felt before. My loveless childhood had not prepared me for the intense love I felt for Rosa, and it was for her sake that I did my best to make Adriana happy so that we could provide a secure family for our daughter.'

Salvatore moved to the window and stared out at the estate's vineyards, stretching away to the horizon. He was proud of his Sicilian heritage. Perhaps it was because his father had sent him away to school that he loved his home so deeply, he thought. He sensed that Darcey was waiting for him to explain more about his marriage, and in a way it was a relief to be able to talk about the past that for four years had been blocked out by his amnesia.

'Adriana hated living at Torre d'Aquila and wanted us to move to Rome. It was the one thing I could not bear to do, even to save my marriage. My heart belongs here,' he said gruffly. 'The vineyards, the rich soil that produces the best grapes—this land is part of me. When I was a boy and my father sent me away to school I felt dead inside, and I did not feel alive again until I returned to the estate. After I finished studying viticulture at university I came back to take charge of the winery and I vowed I would never live anywhere else.'

Salvatore glanced at Darcey and felt his stomach clench with desire. She looked incredibly sexy in the dress he had chosen and his mind was distracted by the erotic fantasy of undressing her. But she deserved to hear the full story, so he continued.

'Adriana returned to her modelling career when Rosa was a few months old. She frequently went away on assignments and left Rosa behind at the castle with me and a nanny. I was concerned that as Rosa grew older she would miss her mother. And then through modelling Adriana came to the notice of a film director who offered her a role in a film. She was determined to move to California to pursue an acting career.'

His jaw tightened. 'It seemed a grim irony that history was repeating itself. My mother had abandoned me to be an actress in America, and now my wife planned to do the same thing and abandon our daughter. That's what we were arguing about when we drove away from the party. For Rosa's sake I begged Adriana to reconsider her plans. She accused me of being selfish and trying to ruin her chance to be an actress—and she was right,' he said heavily. 'If I had been more understanding of Adriana's dreams, if I had agreed to leave Sicily and go to California with her, then she would not have driven off in a temper and lost control of the car—and Rosa would still have a mother.'

'You can't keep blaming yourself,' Darcey said softly. She walked over to Salvatore and placed her hand on his arm. 'For Rosa's sake you have to let go of the past and move on with your life.'

'It will be easier to do so now that I can remember what happened that night.'

He covered her hand with his much larger one and the contact of his warm skin sent a quiver of sensation along

Darcey's arm as she remembered the feel of his naked body on hers when he had made love to her.

'It is thanks to you that I discovered how Lydia and Ettore had tricked me into believing that I was responsible for Adriana's death,' Salvatore told her. 'After we made love last night my amnesia lifted. You have given me my life back. For the first time in four years I can look forward to the future, and I plan to be the best father I can be to Rosa.' He lifted his hand to Darcey's face and looked deeply into her eyes. 'But my immediate plan is to take you to bed and spend the night making love to you, my sweet Darcey.'

He did not mention what would happen *after* they had spent the night together. Darcey had no idea whether she featured in his plans for the future or whether he simply wanted to have sex with her. But her treacherous body did not care. Last night Salvatore had revealed her deeply sensual nature and she had surprised herself with her wanton response to him. Now, as he brushed his lips along her collarbone and found the pulse beating erratically at the base of her throat, molten desire swept through her and the heavy ache in the pit of her stomach became an insistent throb of need.

His lips continued upwards, trailing feather-soft kisses over her face, her eyelids, until finally he claimed her mouth in a fiercely passionate kiss that sent fire coursing through Darcey's veins. She responded to him mindlessly, parting her lips so that he could explore her with his tongue. Nothing mattered except that he should make love to her. Salvatore had not made any promises of wanting a meaningful relationship. But her ex-husband had broken every one of his marriage vows, she thought ruefully. She did not know if she could completely trust any man ever again. Promises were easy to make and easy to break, whereas sexual desire was simple and uncomplicated.

'*Dio*, you drive me insane,' Salvatore said thickly.

But instead of kissing her again, as Darcey had hoped, he stepped away from her and raked a hand through his hair.

'I had the evening planned, but I only have to look at you and all my good intentions disappear.' He lifted her hand to his mouth and brushed his lips across her fingers before leading her over to the table that she saw had been decorated with flowers and candles. 'I planned this evening to be a date,' Salvatore explained. 'Over dinner I thought we could get to know each other better. I don't just want to have sex with you,' he said softly. 'I want to find out more about Darcey Rivers while we eat good food and drink fine wine—but I warn you that we might not make it as far as dessert before my need to make love to you wins over my attempts to be chivalrous,' he admitted ruefully.

Her smile stole his breath. 'I would love to go on a date with you,' Darcey assured him. 'And I'll be quite happy to forgo dessert,' she added, her green eyes shimmering with sensual promise.

A selection of salad dishes, accompanied by cold meats, seafood and cheeses, had been prepared for them, and to go with the food Salvatore served a rich red wine from the Castellano vineyards. The view from the tower of the sun sinking below the horizon was spectacular and Darcey felt relaxed—yet at the same time she felt a shiver of anticipation when she caught the sultry gleam in Salvatore's eyes.

'Tell me more about your family,' he invited. 'You said you are close to your parents? What do they do for a living?'

She hesitated. It was unlikely that her famous family were well known in Sicily, but she had met Salvatore in London and there was a good chance he might have heard of the Hart acting dynasty. If she told him who she was he would probably ask why she had not followed the family tradition and become an actress. She did not want to admit that one reason why she hadn't was because of her lack of self-confidence and her fear that she was not as talented as her parents and siblings. Performing in her father's play would be a big test. Even though the opening night was months away she felt nervous every time she thought about it, and she did not feel confident enough with Salvatore to reveal her insecurities to him.

'My parents own their own business,' she murmured. It was the truth, for her parents still took an active part in running the theatre company they had established when Darcey was a child. 'My father makes wine for a hobby and he has a vineyard at our house in France.' She nudged the conversation in a different direction.

'Really?' Salvatore was immediately curious. 'How many hectares of vines does he have?'

'Um…about three.'

He looked amused. 'Ah, so it's a small-scale winery? There are one hundred hectares of vines on the Castellano Estate. But France certainly produces some of the best wine in the world.'

'*This* is a lovely wine.' Darcey took a sip of the red wine and found it delightfully smooth. 'I think it would be easy to drink too much of it.' She felt light-headed after half a glass, although that might have more to do with the tangible sexual awareness simmering in the tower room, she acknowledged.

She looked across the table at Salvatore and her stomach muscles tightened when she saw the undisguised hunger in his eyes.

'*Darcey!*'

His feral growl sent a shiver of excitement through her. He stood up and walked around the table. Holding out his hand, he drew her to her feet and pulled her into his arms.

'*Carissima*, I have never needed anyone in my life, but I need you,' he said roughly. 'I adore talking to you, but if I don't make love to you right now I think I'll explode.'

His raw honesty moved her. He had tried to keep his tone light, but beneath it she had heard something in his voice that made her imagine him as a lonely boy, abandoned by his mother and sent away to school in a foreign country by his father.

'I think conversation is overrated,' she whispered as she reached up and wound her arms around his neck.

Laughter rumbled in his chest, but there was nothing teasing about his kiss when he claimed her mouth. He pushed his tongue between her lips in an erotic imitation of how he would soon push his powerful erection into her receptive body. Heat pulsed between Darcey's legs and she kissed him with a desperate fervency, trying to show him that her need was as great as his.

While they had been having dinner night had fallen, and outside the sky had darkened to indigo, lit by a huge moon that filled the tower room with silver shadows. Salvatore led Darcey over to an antique *chaise longue* upholstered in rich burgundy velvet and her pulse quickened when she realised that he intended to make love to her on it. He slid the straps of her dress over her shoulders, and when her breasts spilled into his hands he cupped the soft mounds and stroked her nipples until they hardened.

'You are so beautiful,' he whispered against her skin as he trailed his lips over her trembling body.

He took one taut peak into his mouth and suckled her. The sensation was so intense that Darcey gave a soft cry, and when he turned his attention to her other breast she felt molten heat pool between her legs. She was impatient for him to push her down onto the sofa, but he seemed determined to kiss every inch of her body and tugged her dress down so that it settled in a froth of chiffon at her feet. The sight of her lacy thong brought a growl of approval from him as he knelt in front of her and kissed her flat stomach, the soft skin of her inner thighs.

'Salvatore…!' She gave a startled cry when he pressed his mouth to the tiny strip of lace between her legs and then eased the thong to one side so that he could run his tongue up and down her moist opening.

She clutched his shoulders as she felt him gently part her and push his tongue into her to bestow the most intimate caress of all. It was a new experience for Darcey, but her shock quickly turned to pleasure as he brought her to the edge of ecstasy.

'Please…' she gasped, feeling the coiling sensation in her pelvis tighten as Salvatore flicked his tongue across her clitoris.

Her husky plea tugged on Salvatore's heart. Darcey was so sweetly responsive. She had crept under his guard and warmed the coldness inside him, and his sole aim was to please her. Ignoring the urgent need to seek his own satisfaction, he pressed his mouth against the heart of her femininity and tasted the sensual musk of her arousal.

The storm inside her was building, and Darcey could feel her control slipping. She dug her nails into Salvatore's shoulders as he continued to pleasure her with his wickedly invasive tongue. She needed to tell him that if he didn't stop she would—

'Oh...'

Her thought-processes juddered to a halt as the first ripples of orgasm swiftly intensified until her entire body pulsed with pleasure. Only then, when she was gasping and her legs buckled, did Salvatore lift her in his arms and place her on the velvet cushions of the *chaise longue*. She watched him strip, her heart thumping, and when he stood between her legs she arched her hips and gave a choked cry as he plunged his powerful erection deep into her.

He filled her, completed her, and with every hard stroke he claimed possession of her body and her soul. Her second orgasm was even more intense than her first, and as she wrapped her legs around his back he gave the hardest thrust yet and his body shuddered with the force of his release.

A long time afterwards Salvatore lifted his head from the soft pillow of Darcey's breasts and looked into her bright green eyes. 'Not only was your husband a jerk, but he was evidently a selfish lover too. Didn't he ever take the time to discover ways to give you pleasure?'

She flushed, feeling embarrassed that he had guessed oral sex was a new experience for her. 'The truth is my marriage was shaky right from the start,' she admitted. 'I found out soon after the wedding that Marcus had only married me because...'

Her voice faltered. She felt reluctant to admit the humiliating truth that Marcus had married her because he had wanted to get close to her famous family.

'I wasn't the person Marcus thought I was,' she said at last. 'We met while we were staying at the same beach resort, and I think we were both seduced by the romantic atmosphere. But I should have known that holiday romances don't last. The reality of living together re-

vealed how unsuited we were. I wasn't exciting enough
for Marcus.'

The faint tremor in her voice made Salvatore wonder
if she still had feelings for her ex-husband, and he was
surprised by how strongly he disliked the idea. He knew
Darcey was an intensely loyal person, but he was certain
that any residual feelings she might feel for the man she
had married were misplaced.

'Let me show you how very exciting I find you, *mia
bella*,' he murmured, shifting his position so that his
erection nudged between her legs.

He loved the way her eyes darkened to jade with desire. Her soft smile as she took him inside her tugged
on his heart. He was still coming to terms with regain-
ing his memory and finally discovering the truth about
the accident. But for the first time in four years he was
able to look forward, and the future suddenly seemed
full of promise.

CHAPTER TEN

SALVATORE FELT A surge of pleasure when he walked across the lawn and saw Darcey sitting beneath the shade of a parasol. She was wearing a simple white shift dress that showed off her light golden tan. Her silky bob of copper-brown hair framed her lovely face and she looked elegant, innocent, and incredibly sexy all at once.

His sense of well-being increased when he leaned down to claim her mouth and she parted her lips for him to deepen the kiss.

'You seem to be permanently attached to your laptop.' His light tone did not fully disguise his curiosity about why she spent so much of her free time when she wasn't with Rosa working on her computer.

Darcey considered explaining that for the past few weeks she had been studying the role she was to take in her father's play, but talking about it would make it real, and for the sake of her edgy nerves she preferred not to think about the opening night, when she would walk onto the stage for the first time. Looking beyond the play, she had written a business proposal that she hoped would convince the bank to give her a loan so she could set up a private speech therapy practice.

Salvatore glanced over her shoulder at the columns of figures on the screen.

'I need to make my business plan impressive so that the bank will agree to lend me enough money to cover the initial expense of setting up a private speech therapy clinic,' she told him. 'I've never run my own business before and it's all a bit daunting.'

'I'll take a look at your proposal, if you like. I'm busy at the moment, with the grape harvest, but there's no hurry, is there? I thought you were planning to start your business some time next year?'

The shutters had come down on Salvatore's expression so that Darcey had no idea what he was thinking. She wondered why he had offered to look at the proposal when he clearly wasn't interested. His tone was cool, almost off-hand, reminding her of how aloof he had been when she had first met him.

'I need to have my plans ready. Time passes so quickly. It's September already, and I'll be going home at the end of the month.' The thought made her heart ache, and in an effort to disguise the huskiness in her voice she said quickly, 'I've been thinking about who you could employ to replace me as Rosa's speech therapist, and I've had an idea. A colleague I used to work with retired from her job last year, but she still does some private work. Pamela doesn't have any family ties and I'm sure she would agree to come to Sicily and work with Rosa.'

'We'll discuss the matter another time,' Salvatore told her in a noncommittal voice. 'Has Rosa told you that she is going to stay at Casa Camelia for a couple of days, while I go to Rome for a business meeting?'

'Yes, she's very excited about her first sleepover with her cousin. Although I'm not sure how much sleep the children will actually get—or Sergio and Kristen, for that matter.' Darcey gave him a rueful look. 'If you had asked me, I would have been happy to look after Rosa. I didn't know until she told me at breakfast that you were going away.'

She could not hide the note of hurt in her voice that Salvatore hadn't informed her of his plans. His desire for her showed no sign of fading, and he made love to her every night with tenderness as well as passion, so that she had started to hope that perhaps he cared for her, but the fact that he had not deemed it necessary to tell her about his trip to Rome was a clear indication that he did not have any regard for her or her feelings.

He brushed a few strands of hair back from her face and his expression softened. 'That is because Rosa was sworn to secrecy. I arranged for her to stay with Sergio and Kristen because you are coming to Rome with me.'

The warmth in his eyes set her pulse racing. 'Why would you want to take me to a business meeting?'

'I'll leave you while I meet with my export manager, but the meeting shouldn't take more than a couple of hours—enough time for you to investigate the shoe shops on Via Condotti. We'll have lunch at a restaurant and spend the afternoon exploring the city. I overheard you telling Armond that you would love to visit the Colosseum,' he murmured.

'But you are so busy with the harvest. I'm sure you don't have time to take me on a sightseeing trip.'

'I always have time for you, *carissima*.' Salvatore could not resist the temptation of Darcey's soft lips and he kissed her again, a slow, drugging kiss tinged with the tenderness he felt for her. 'It will be good for us to spend some time together. There's something I want to talk to you about.'

Whatever he wanted to talk about sounded serious, Darcey thought nervously. 'Rosa has already gone to Casa Camelia. We have time to talk now,' she suggested.

'No, we don't. We're leaving on the helicopter in fifteen minutes.'

'But I need to pack for the trip…'

She jumped to her feet, but as she was about to race into the castle Salvatore slipped his arm around her waist.

'Everything has been taken care of. I asked the maid to pack for you. All you have to do is relax and enjoy yourself. You've worked so hard with Rosa, and her speech is improving amazingly fast. This trip is a way for me to show you how much I appreciate all that you have done for my daughter—and for me,' Salvatore said, his voice roughening with emotions that until he had met Darcey had been unfamiliar to him. 'For the next few days and nights I intend to devote myself to you, *mia bella*. Especially the nights,' he added, giving her a wolfish smile that made her pulse-rate rocket.

It was Darcey's first visit to Rome, and she discovered a bustling, cosmopolitan city with a fascinating historical heritage. She had assured Salvatore that she would be fine on her own while he attended his business meeting.

On his way out of their hotel room he'd pulled her into his arms and kissed her hard, as if he was reluctant to leave her. 'I'll cancel my meeting,' he'd said gruffly.

'You can't. Your business is important.' She had pushed away the thought that she would miss him even for a few hours. 'I'll be waiting for you,' she'd told him, with a sweet smile that tugged on Salvatore's insides.

At lunchtime she found the restaurant close to the landmark Spanish Steps where she had arranged to meet him and was informed that Salvatore had not yet arrived, but their table was ready. As she followed the waiter outside to a pretty courtyard filled with the scent of roses and orange blossom she guessed his meeting had overrun, but she was happy to sit and sip a glass of lemonade while she studied the restaurant's clientele.

It was obviously a popular place for local Romans to dine. The women were sophisticated, and most of the men were wearing suits and looked like successful business-men. Take the man who had just stepped into the court-yard. He was impeccably dressed in a pale grey suit and dark blue silk shirt, and was so stunningly handsome that it was impossible not to notice him. His almost black hair gleamed like raw silk and was cut short in a style that emphasised his chiselled cheekbones and square jaw.

Darcey's heart missed a beat as the man headed pur-posefully in her direction and she realised why he seemed familiar.

'I'm sorry I'm late, *carissima*.'

She could not stop staring at Salvatore. 'You look…' she had been going to say *different* '…gorgeous,' she said huskily. 'Why did you cut your hair?'

His smile blew her away. 'I decided it was time I smartened up my appearance. I have finally put the past behind me. It's time to make a fresh start and look to the future.'

'I'm glad for you.' It was the truth, but Darcey felt as if an arrow had pierced her heart when she thought about *her* future. In a couple of weeks she would go back to London and it was likely that she would never see Salvatore again. He had not suggested that he wanted their affair to continue, and anyway the logis-tics of a long-distance relationship would be difficult— especially while she was rehearsing for her father's play, she thought dully.

She told herself to enjoy the time she had left with him, but although the baked sea bass she had ordered was delicious her appetite had disappeared. After lunch, when

they strolled around Rome visiting the popular tour-
ist sites, she was aware of the interested glances other
women sent him and jealousy burned in her stomach. If
Salvatore's hopes for the future included marrying again
he would have no shortage of candidates willing to share
his life and his bed at Torre d'Aquila.

They returned to the hotel in the early evening.

'I've booked a table for dinner here at the hotel's
restaurant for eight o'clock,' Salvatore said as he followed Darcey into the bedroom of their luxury suite.
He watched her kick off her shoes and frowned when he
noticed her face was unusually pale. 'Why don't you lie
down for a while? It was hot walking around the city and
you're probably tired.'

Salvatore had been a wonderful tour guide, showing
her the famous sights of Rome, and he had gone to a lot
of effort to make the day enjoyable. Darcey did not want
him to think she was unappreciative. It wasn't his fault
she had fallen so deeply in love with him that the thought
of leaving him was tearing her apart, she acknowledged.

She dredged up a smile. 'I'm not at all tired.'

Her heart thudded when he drew her into his arms.
'In that case you definitely need to lie down, *cara*,' he
murmured, his voice as sensuous as crushed velvet. 'We
have a few hours to spare until dinner and I have an excellent idea for how we can use the time.'

He bent his head and claimed her mouth, the kiss
quickly changing from gentle to fiercely passionate as
Darcey responded to him with an urgency that set them
both alight. She could not resist him—not when she knew
that soon there would be no more chances to make love
with him. She would go back to London and he would
remain at his castle, free at last from the darkness of his
past and ready to move on with his life.

Perhaps you should tell him how you feel about him, prompted a voice inside her head. The idea caused Darcey's stomach to lurch. Salvatore had always known that she would be going home at the end of September and he had never asked her to extend her stay. She was no longer worried that he was in love with his dead wife. He had admitted that he had never been in love with Adriana. That was what troubled her. Salvatore had revealed that as a result of his unhappy childhood he found it hard to get close to anyone. If he felt anything at all for her he was keeping his feelings well hidden.

He moved his hands round to her back and ran the zip down her spine. Her dress slithered to the floor, quickly followed by her bra and knickers.

'*Dio*, have you any idea what you do to me?' he demanded hoarsely. 'All day I have thought about holding you like this, undressing you and feeling your naked skin against mine.'

Salvatore might be a master at hiding his emotions, but his undisguised desire for her was balm to Darcey's aching heart. She helped him out of his clothes with unashamed eagerness and they fell onto the bed in a tangle of limbs, their breathing quickening as they touched and stroked each other until the waiting became intolerable and he pulled her beneath him.

He made love to her hard and fast and they climaxed simultaneously. A little while later he rolled onto his back and guided her down onto him. This time the loving was slower and more intense, and as Salvatore groaned and buried his face in Darcey's neck he wondered what the hell was happening to him.

'I don't want your retired friend to take your place as Rosa's speech therapist.'

Darcey was half-asleep, her body utterly relaxed in

the sensuous aftermath of passion. Salvatore had made love to her with such tenderness and exquisite care that tears had filled her eyes and love had filled her heart.

She opened her eyes to find him propped on one elbow, leaning over her. She couldn't get over how gorgeous he looked with his short hair and clean-shaven jaw. But the biggest change was the warmth in his eyes. He had looked so cold and stern when she had first met him, she mused. But now he looked relaxed and unbelievably sexy.

She tried to concentrate on what he had said.

'Pamela Dickens has years of experience in speech therapy, and she is a very kind person. I think Rosa would like her,' she said, guessing that he was concerned about how Rosa would react to a new therapist.

'You don't understand.'

He held her gaze, and something in his expression made Darcey's heart miss a beat.

'I don't want you to go back to London. I want you to stay at Torre d'Aquila with Rosa—and with me.'

'Salvatore, I…' She was prevented from saying anything more when he placed his finger across her lips.

'I was going to say this over dinner, but as usual you have turned my plans upside down,' he said wryly. 'I know you want to set up a private practice, but maybe you could put your plans on hold. I understand that your career is important to you.' His voice deepened. 'But *you* are important to me, Darcey.'

Salvatore could feel his heart slamming against his ribs. He could not remember ever feeling nervous in his life and it was not a comfortable experience. But he had realised that he could not let Darcey walk out of his life.

'There is something special between us. I think,' he said. 'I'd hoped that you feel it too, *carissima*.'

Darcey's breath was trapped in her lungs and her voice emerged as a whisper. 'What exactly are you saying?'

'I'm asking you if you will live at the castle with me instead of going back to England and let's see how our relationship develops.'

His hand was unsteady as he brushed Darcey's hair back from her face. The emotions she evoked in him were unlike anything he had felt for any other woman and he was still trying to assimilate what it was he felt for her.

'I don't know what is ahead for us,' he told her honestly. 'All I know is that before I met you I gave no thought to the future, but now I don't want to contemplate a future without you.'

It was not a declaration of love, but Salvatore's confession that she was special to him was more than Darcey had dared to hope for. Was it enough for her to alter her career plans and leave her family and friends to move to Sicily? It could be the biggest gamble of her life, she acknowledged. But if she walked away from him without giving their relationship a chance she knew she would regret it for the rest of her life.

She curled her arms around his neck and pulled his mouth down to hers. 'I'll stay on one condition,' she murmured.

His shoulders tensed. 'And what is that?'

'That you promise to make love to me as beautifully as you did a few minutes ago at least once a night.'

Salvatore felt a gentle tug on his heart as he stared into her bright green eyes. 'I give you my word, *cara.*' He grinned, feeling more carefree than he had ever done. 'And there's a good chance I'll manage mornings and possibly afternoons too,' he murmured.

The teasing and the underlying tenderness between them was new to him. His upbringing had taught him not to analyse his emotions, but if he'd had to describe how he felt right now, *happy* summed up his feelings perfectly, Salvatore mused.

'I will still have to go home for a couple of months,' Darcey said ruefully. 'I can't let my father down. But I'll come back to Torre d'Aquila after...' She hesitated.

'After what?' Salvatore trailed his lips over her throat. He did not want to talk, he wanted to make love to her, but something in her tone made him lift his head and look at her. 'Why do you need to return to London?'

'Well...' Darcey took a deep breath. Salvatore would be the only person outside of her family to know that she was going to perform in her father's play, and it was a measure of how much she trusted him that she felt comfortable to talk to him about it. 'I'm going to take the lead role in a play my father has written. You might have heard of the actor and playwright Joshua Hart?'

Salvatore frowned. 'He is a renowned English Shakespearean actor. I actually saw him play Hamlet at the Globe Theatre last year, when I was in London.' He gave her a puzzled look. 'The Hart family are well known in the theatrical world. But what does that have to do with you?'

'Joshua is my father. Hart was my maiden name.'

He stared at her. His brain seemed to have frozen. He couldn't think and he was sure he could not have heard Darcey correctly.

'Are you saying that you're family are *actors*?' His brain unfroze. 'And *you* are going to act in a play?'

It did not make sense. She was a speech therapist, for God's sake!

He sat up and raked a hand through his hair. 'Let me get this straight. *You intend to leave me because you want to pursue a career as an actress.*' He gave a bitter laugh. 'Well, there's nothing new there. First my mother left because she dreamed of becoming a film star, then my wife, and now you.'

'*No*, it's not like that at all,' Darcey said urgently. It had not crossed her mind that Salvatore would link her decision to perform in the play with his mother's and Adriana's determination to be an actress. But now that he had pointed it out she felt guilty that she had not told him about her connection to the acting world. 'I don't want to be a film star. I'm not even a proper actress, although I did a bit of acting when I was younger. I decided that I wanted a different career to the rest of my family.'

Darcey's voice faded as she watched get up from the bed and pull his trousers on. His jaw was set, but she did not understand why he was angry. The happiness she had felt a few moments ago was trickling away as fast as sand in an egg-timer.

'I agreed to take this particular role because the play is about my grandmother and is very personal to my father,' she explained hurriedly. 'The production is only booked to run for two months.'

'What will happen if the play is a success and continues to run?'

'I suppose another actress will take the lead role.'

'And your father wouldn't persuade you to carry on playing the part indefinitely? There is a play in the West End that has run for more than twenty years.'

'I think it's unlikely that Dad's play will be as successful as *The Mousetrap*.' Darcey sighed. 'Look, I realise this is a surprise…'

'That's something of an understatement,' Salvatore said with savage sarcasm. 'Why didn't you mention before about your connection to the acting profession? You deliberately kept it a secret. You even lied to me when

I asked you what your parents did for a living. You said they own a business.'

She flushed. 'I didn't lie. My parents run a theatre company called Speak Out, which aims to bring drama to the deaf community. When I was growing up I used to perform with the company. My father was disappointed when I decided not to carry on acting. I agreed to be in this play because…well, to be honest I wanted to please him,' Darcey admitted huskily. 'Dad and I have had a bit of a rocky relationship since I decided to train as a speech therapist rather than go to drama school. I hoped that working together on the play would bring us closer.'

Salvatore's eyes were as black and hard as basalt spewed from Mount Etna. 'All this time you have hidden who you really are.'

'I didn't tell you about my family because I've had past experiences where people have tried to befriend me just because my name is Hart. That was especially true of my ex-husband.' She took a deep breath. She had never told anyone the humiliating truth about her marriage, but she wanted to be honest with Salvatore. 'Marcus is an actor, with his sights set on stardom. He told me he was in love with me, but I found out after the wedding that he had only pretended to be interested in me because he thought that having Joshua Hart as a father-in-law would help his career.'

'So you didn't trust me?'

Salvatore's words fell into the room like pebbles hitting the surface of a pool.

'I…' Darcey swallowed, unable to deny the accusation.

'Dio!' he exploded. 'I have turned my insides out and bared my soul to you, and you couldn't even tell me your goddamned *name*.'

'I'm sorry,' she mumbled. 'After what Marcus did I

have found it hard to trust people. But I *do* trust you, and I very much want to come back to Sicily when the play is finished and…and live with you and Rosa.'

'You say now that you'll come back, but my past experiences suggest that the lure of fame is hard to resist,' Salvatore said bitterly. 'Perhaps you would find living at the castle boring after being on the stage?'

His jaw clenched.

'My mother abandoned me when I was five years old because she wanted to be a famous film star, and for the same reason my wife planned to abandon our baby daughter. Rosa has already grown close to you. How can you simply walk away from her and let her think that you don't care? But maybe you don't give a damn about her?'

Maybe she didn't give a damn about *him*, Salvatore thought grimly. Maybe she had been acting all these weeks that they had been lovers. Perhaps her soft smile and the way she whispered his name when he made love to her hadn't been signs that she cared for him—*as he cared for her*. The realisation of how much he cared hit him so hard that it sucked the breath out of him.

'Of course I care about Rosa,' Darcey said strongly.

'Then why are you going to abandon her?'

Why are you going to abandon me?

The unspoken question circled in his mind and memories of his childhood came rushing back. He remembered when he was five years old. Remembered his father telling him that his mother had gone away for ever and taken his twin brother with her.

Salvatore hadn't believed it. His mother had gone away before, to act in films, but she had always come back. He had run upstairs to her bedroom and flung open the wardrobes. Each one had been empty. Patti's clothes had all gone and all that had remained in the room was the lingering scent of her perfume. To this day the fragrance of lilies brought a lump to his throat.

He had gone to find Sergio, to tell him that Mamma had left them. His father must have been playing a trick on him when he'd said that his brother had gone too. But Sergio had not been in the nursery, or in the garden. Salvatore had searched the whole estate for his brother before he'd realised that he really was alone, abandoned, and his heart had felt as if it was breaking.

But it had not broken, of course. Hearts did not really break—it was just an expression people used.

'You're not being fair to Rosa. Even if you came back to the castle after this play you might go away again if another role came up. She has had enough instability in her life. I can't risk you hurting her.'

'I swear that won't happen,' Darcey told him intently.

'Then tell your father that you can't take this role.'

'I can't do that. I made a promise to him and I won't let him down.'

'But you don't care about letting *me* down?' Salvatore said harshly. 'A few moments ago you agreed to stay with me and give our relationship a chance, but you are determined to put your father's wishes above mine.'

'It is not only for my father's sake that I want to do the play,' Darcey admitted. 'I want to do it for me. I was never as self-confident as the other members of my family. After my divorce I felt even worse because Marcus had made a fool of me. The play is a chance to prove to myself that I can be strong and brave and face my fears. But that is nothing compared to the bravery my grandmother showed during the war, and I feel honoured that my father chose me to tell her story.'

She met Salvatore's bitter black gaze and her heart sank.

'I promise I'll come back to you.'

She could feel him putting up barriers and shutting her out.

'Trust works both ways,' she said quietly. 'You have to trust that I will keep my word, and if you can't, then...'

'Then what, Darcey?' he challenged.

The question hung in the air between them. Darcey recalled Kristen's warning that Castellano men could be very stubborn. It seemed that Salvatore only wanted a relationship with her on his terms and wasn't prepared to compromise.

'If you can't trust me, then there can be no future for us.'

Her mouth felt dry with the fear that she was killing their relationship stone-dead. If she agreed to pull out of the play everything would be all right, but what would happen the next time they disagreed about something? Would she have to give in to him to keep the peace between them?

Salvatore was such a strong character, and sometimes she felt overwhelmed by him. He could very easily dominate her and she was scared by how desperately she loved him. She wanted to please him—just as she had always wanted to please her father, she thought with a flash of insight. The truth was she needed to go away for a while and put some distance between her and Salvatore while she came to terms with her feelings for him. But, even though she knew it was the right thing to do, her heart ached at the idea of leaving him and Rosa even for a few weeks.

'I have explained why doing the play is important to me,' she said huskily. 'But if you won't even wait for me for a couple of months then it makes me wonder if I am really as special to you as you said, or whether that's a line you spin to all your mistresses.'

Salvatore stiffened. So she still intended to leave? He shouldn't be surprised, he told himself. She had obviously never cared about him. It was lucky he hadn't told her that he—*Dio!* What a fool he had been to think that she might have loved him.

He shrugged. 'It seems that neither of us have been completely honest, doesn't it, *cara*?'

He made the endearment sound like an insult. It was impossible to believe that his eyes had ever gleamed with sensual passion, let alone tenderness, Darcey thought dully.

She felt numb inside as she watched him stride over to the door. 'Where are you going?'

'I need some air.' He glanced back at her and his hard features did not alter when he saw her lower lip tremble. 'You need to make a choice, Darcey. Stay with me—or walk away for ever.'

CHAPTER ELEVEN

HE WALKED WITHOUT knowing where he was going, without caring. The crowds on the streets were thinning in the evening; the restaurants and bars were busy. By the Trevi Fountain he saw two lovers entwined in each other's arms, oblivious to the world. *Enjoy it while it lasts*, he thought cynically. And the ache inside him grew heavier.

When he reached the river the sun was sinking below the horizon and the lamps that lined the riverbank cast their golden light on the dark water. There was peace here—solitude for a man who was always alone. Maybe it was his destiny, but it felt like a curse.

His steps slowed as he recalled the past weeks, when he hadn't been lonely. Darcey had lit up the castle and his life with her beautiful smile and her sheer joy in living. He had never laughed so much as he had since she had come to Torre d'Aquila. He had not laughed much at all before he had met her, Salvatore acknowledged. He had not known what it truly meant to make love until he had looked into her eyes as their two bodies became one and felt complete for the first time in his life.

He carried on walking, but without the same urgency, without the anger. Why was he so angry because she wanted to go back to England for a few weeks? he asked himself. She had said that performing in her father's play was important to her, and rather than assuring her that he understood he had tried to manipulate her and control her instead of listening to her.

The truth was that he *was* afraid that if she left she would not come back—as his mother hadn't. He was afraid of being hurt. And so to disguise his fear he had said awful things to her and told her she had to choose between what she wanted and what he wanted. Instead of opening his heart to her he had issued her with a god-damned ultimatum.

Madonna—what had he done? He turned on his heel and began to walk back the way he had come, back to the hotel.

'If you can't trust me...'

Her words echoed inside his head and the black shadows from his past lifted. Of course he trusted her. She had proved over and over that she kept her word. She had worked diligently to help his daughter learn to speak, and her patience and loving care had already transformed Rosa into a happy and confident child. His heart clenched. Darcey would not abandon Rosa, and she would not abandon him, but he feared that he might have driven her away.

He began to run, ignoring the pain in his injured leg. He ran all the way back to the hotel. When he entered their suite and saw that the wardrobe where she had hung her clothes was empty the pain of his heart breaking was the worst agony he'd ever experienced, and the lingering scent of jasmine and old-fashioned roses brought a lump to his throat.

Darcey's father had once told her that sitting alone in a dressing room in the final minutes before a performance were the longest and loneliest moments of an actor's life. Now she knew how true his words were, she brooded as she watched the hands on the clock move excruciatingly slowly.

Her nerves were jangling and she just wanted to get the first night over with. She must have been mad to agree to do this. She must have been crazy to walk away from Salvatore. She loved him, so why hadn't she stayed?

Because he doesn't love you, said the voice in her head. He had proved that when he had told her to choose. *'Stay with me—or walk away for ever.'*

The weeks since she had returned to London had flown past. She was glad that rehearsals had taken up so much of her time, because concentrating on her role had prevented her from thinking about Salvatore. But it was a different matter when she went home every evening. She had spent the first few days after she'd arrived home clinging to the hope that he would phone. That hope had long since died, and her anger at his intransigence had also faded. Now she simply felt guilty that she had not told him sooner about her intention to perform in the play, and her heart felt like a lead weight in her chest.

Her father had commented on her weight loss, which had left her looking gaunt, while her sleepless nights were evident in the dark circles beneath her eyes.

'I know your grandmother often went without food when she worked for the French Resistance, and I commend your dedication to portraying Edith realistically, but I really wish you would eat properly,' Joshua had said in concern.

Salvatore might retract his accusation that she hankered for fame and glamour if he saw her in the drab trench coat she wore for most of the performance, Darcey thought ruefully. The play was not a West End production and was being staged at a fringe theatre in Islington. But a Joshua Hart play was guaranteed to draw interest from the media, and Darcey knew that several respected theatre critics were in the audience.

A knock on the dressing room door caused her stomach to cramp with nerves. Taking a deep breath, she managed to smile at the assistant stage manager.

'This was delivered for you,' he said, handing her a long cardboard box.

Her parents and other family members had already sent her bouquets of flowers to wish her luck. Darcey fumbled with the ribbon and opened the box to reveal a single red rose.

'Do you know who sent it?' she asked shakily. 'There's no note with the box.'

The ASM shook his head. 'All I know it that someone left it at the front desk a few minutes ago. They were cutting it fine—the play is about to start.' He smiled at her. 'Are you ready, Miss Hart?'

She lifted the rose and smelled its exquisite perfume. Strangely, she did not feel nervous any more. She could do this, Darcey told herself. For her father, but more importantly, for herself.

'Yes,' she said steadily. 'I'm ready.'

'Did you know that the critics from most of the national papers were here tonight, and all of them have given your performance fantastic reviews?' Joshua Hart told Darcey as he steered her across the packed room where the after-show party was taking place. 'I've always known you are a gifted actress. It's in your blood. And tonight you've proved that you are a true Hart.' His tone became serious. 'You could have a wonderful acting career. But it's not what you want, is it?' he said intuitively.

Darcey shook her head. 'I'm happy with the career I've chosen. I'm sorry, Dad.'

Her father looked surprised. 'You have nothing to apologise for. I'm proud of you—*and* the job you do.' He looked at her closely. 'Are you all right? Your mother thought there was some chap in Sicily...'

'I'm fine,' she said quickly.

It was untrue, of course. From the moment she had walked onto the stage and searched along the front row of the audience she had been far from fine. Her hopes that Salvatore had sent her the red rose and come to see the play had been dashed and she had been dangerously close to tears for the whole performance. She had been stupid to think that he might use the ticket she had posted to him, she told herself.

The brief note she had sent with it to the castle had been her only communication with him since he had stormed out of their hotel room in Rome. Furious at his uncompromising attitude, she had gone straight down to the reception desk and arranged to catch the next flight back to London.

If she had stayed would they have been able to discuss things rationally once they had cooled down? She would never know, and regret deepened Darcey's misery so that it took all her acting skills to smile and chat with the other members of the cast.

The party ended eventually, but the prospect of driving through the dank November night to her empty house was so depressing that she hung around until she was the last person left in the theatre.

She walked across the stage and stared out at the dark auditorium. There was no one there to see her tears and she could not hold them back any longer. She had a lot to look forward to, she tried to convince herself. The bank had agreed to give her a loan, and in the new year she intended to look for premises where she could establish a private speech therapy clinic.

Footsteps rang out hollowly in the empty theatre. Alfred, the caretaker, probably wanted to lock up.

'I thought you would be celebrating your success.'

The gravelly, achingly familiar voice tore at her heart. Her eyes flew open and she blinked to clear her blurred vision.

'Wh…what are *you* doing here?'

Salvatore stepped out of the shadows and Darcey felt a sharp pang of physical awareness as she studied his chiselled features. His hair was cut short, like the last time she had seen him, and the grey wool overcoat he was wearing over a black silk shirt emphasised his powerful athletic build. He looked less like a pirate and more like a billionaire businessman. Darcey thought he looked utterly gorgeous.

'Where else would I be?' he murmured. 'I wouldn't have missed your first night for the world.'

'That wasn't the impression you gave in Rome.'

She brushed her tears away, unaware that Salvatore's gut clenched as he saw the betraying tremble of her hand.

'I was a bloody fool in Rome.'

He walked down the centre aisle of the auditorium and Darcey noticed that he limped heavily.

'Your leg…?'

He shrugged. 'The damp weather plays hell with the metal pins holding my thigh bone together, but I'll live,' he said drily. 'The opening night of your play coincided with a trip I'd planned to make to London. I'm selling the house on Park Lane.'

'I suppose there's no point in keeping it now that Rosa no longer needs to see the audiologist at the hospital?'

'I intend to buy another house—preferably on the outskirts of London. I'm looking for a family home.' He gave her a wry look. 'With less marble features and a garden for Rosa to play in. She misses you,' he said quietly.

Darcey bit her lip. 'I miss her too.'

'Actually, I have a shortlist of properties to view,' Salvatore continued. 'I was hoping you would come and look at them with me.'

Being so close to him was sheer torture—especially when all he seemed to want to discuss was the property market. Darcey closed her eyes and felt hot tears seep beneath her lashes.

'I'm sure an estate agent will be able to advise you much better than I can.' Her voice cracked. 'Look, I don't know why you want to buy a house in London when your home and your heart are in Sicily.'

She could not stop crying, and she felt such an idiot. Angry with herself, she turned to walk into the wings. But Salvatore leapt up onto the stage and caught hold of her, spinning her round to face him. His dark eyes blazed with an expression that made her catch her breath.

'My heart is wherever you are,' he said fiercely. 'I'm buying a house in England for you, *carissima*, for *us*—if you will have me.'

'I don't understand.' Her voice was choked with tears. 'You were so furious. I understand why you thought I had betrayed you. I should have told you that I come from a famous acting family, and that I had accepted a role in my father's play. I should have trusted that you are nothing like Marcus. But in the past people have wanted to get close to me just because of my family, and I liked the fact that you wanted to be with me for who I am.'

Salvatore exhaled heavily. 'When you said you were returning to London to be an actress it felt like history was repeating itself yet again. All I could think of was that you were going to leave me, like my mother had left and Adriana had planned to do, because the life I had offered you in Sicily was not as exciting as a career as a film star. It hurt to know that you had kept secrets from me,' he admitted roughly. 'It shames me to say that my anger made me want to hurt you. After I'd stormed out of the hotel I regretted behaving the way I had, and especially giving you an ultimatum to choose between me and performing in the play. I had behaved like an arrogant jerk and I realised that I needed to do some serious thinking about our relationship and how I really felt about you.'

He brushed the tears from her cheeks with gentle fingers. Darcey's heart gave a jolt when she saw his soft expression. How *did* he really feel about her? She refused to allow herself to hope that just because he had come to see the play she meant something to him. She wished he would be honest, even if that meant telling her that there was no future for them. Then he could go away and leave her alone to deal with her broken heart.

'When I went back to the hotel and found you had gone it was clear that you had made your choice. I knew I could only blame myself for driving you away.' Salvatore's voice cracked as he recalled feeling as if a knife had sliced his heart open when he had discovered that she had left him.

'Since then I have been putting plans into place. I've appointed a manager to run the Castellano winery, and I have helped the castle staff to find new jobs. Only Armond will remain to look after Torre d'Aquila.'

Darcey gave him a startled look. 'But...why won't you be living there? You love the castle and the vineyards.

You told me once that you belong to the land and that you would never live anywhere but the castle.'

'There is no joy at Torre d'Aquila since you left. It's just a pile of ancient bricks—soulless and lifeless without you there.' Salvatore cupped Darcey's chin and tilted her face so that he could look into her tear-bright green eyes. 'When I watched your performance tonight I realised what an incredible talent you have. Your compassion and sensitivity make you a gifted actress, and I don't doubt that after the reviews you've received offers for other acting roles will flood in. That is why I am willing to move to London, or LA—wherever you need to be to develop your acting career.'

Darcey's heart thudded as his words slowly sank in. 'Do you mean you would leave Sicily for me?'

'I would follow you to the ends of the earth if you asked me to.' Salvatore drew a ragged breath. 'Haven't you worked it out by now, sweet Darcey? I love you. Nothing means more to me than your happiness. I don't care where we live so long as your beautiful smile is the first thing I see every morning and I can hold you in my arms every night and make love to you with all the love that is in my heart.'

His mouth twisted when he saw her stunned expression.

'I never knew I could feel like this. I didn't believe I could fall in love. But within five minutes of walking into your office I was determined to take you to Sicily, and even back then I sensed that I would never want to let you go.'

Her silence filled Salvatore with black despair.

'I appreciate your offer to leave Torre d'Aquila—' she began.

He could not bear to hear the rest of her sentence.

'But you don't feel the same way about me—that's what you're going to say, isn't it?' His throat ached and he had to force the words out. 'I should have expected it. I am not an easy man to love.'

'Oh, I don't know,' she said softly. 'I fell in love with you very easily about twenty seconds after you strolled into my office and immediately reorganised my life.'

'Darcey?' Salvatore closed his eyes briefly and when he opened them again his lashes were wet. '*Tesoro*…do you really love me?'

She heard the lonely boy he had once been and her heart cracked open.

'You are everything…my world, the love of my life.' Lost for words to tell him what he meant to her, she framed his face with her hands and drew his mouth down to hers.

It was a kiss unlike any they had shared before. Almost tentative at first, and achingly tender, a silent vow of unending love and the promise of passion as Salvatore took control and kissed her with fierce desire.

'I left because I was scared of how much I love you,' she admitted painfully. 'I thought that if we were apart for a while I would be able to control my feelings for you.' Her voice wobbled. 'But I have missed you so much.'

'*Carissima*, I have missed you desperately, but I wanted you to be able to concentrate on the play and I told myself I must be patient and wait for you. But I can't wait any longer. Will you marry me?' he said urgently. 'We'll need to discuss where we will live, and if you take film roles you'll probably have to go away on location, but I know we can work things out. I love you, and all I want is to make you happy.'

Darcey stood on tiptoe and linked her arms around his neck. 'Then take me home to your castle. I'm pleased to have done this play, but when it finishes I have no intention of taking any more roles. You belong at Torre d'Aquila and I belong with you,' she told him softly. 'What I want more than anything is to be your wife and Rosa's mother. She is going to need speech therapy for a while yet, and I love her as if she were my own child.'

Her smile made Salvatore catch his breath.

'My answer to your question is yes, I'd love to marry you. I hope we'll fill the castle with our children, who will never doubt that we love them as deeply as we love each other.'

Salvatore drew Darcey into his arms and held her close, wondering if she could feel the thunderous beat of his heart. *'Ti amo,'* he said, in a voice choked with emotion.

After a lifetime of burying his feelings he did not find it easy to express how he felt. But he showed her as he claimed her mouth and kissed her with all the love in his heart.

The play finished its run two days before Christmas. Salvatore and Rosa had moved into Darcey's tiny house in London with her and they had lived together as a family. On Christmas Eve they woke to find a thick layer of snow on the ground. It was the first time Rosa had seen snow, and she was wide-eyed with excitement as the car taking her and Darcey to the church drove through the white streets.

Being a bridesmaid was a big responsibility, and the little girl clutched her basket of white rosebuds tightly as she followed Darcey down the aisle to where Papa was waiting. Papa had said that today Darcey was going to become his wife and Rosa's *mamma*. Rosa felt so happy that she gave a little skip and waved to her cousin Nico, who was watching the proceedings with his parents and baby brother.

At the altar Salvatore could not resist turning his head to watch the two people he loved more than anything in the world walk towards him. Rosa looked adorable in her red velvet cloak, but his eyes were drawn to the woman who had stolen his heart. Darcey was breathtaking in a white silk bridal gown edged with pearls at the neckline and the hems of the long sleeves. In her hands she carried a bouquet of red roses, and her only jewellery was the heart-shaped diamond pendant he had given to her, which sparkled in the rays of the winter sunshine.

The wedding ceremony was simple but deeply moving, and the groom's deep voice was unsteady as he made his vows and promised to love his bride for eternity. Soon they would be returning to the castle in Sicily, but Salvatore's heart no longer belonged to Torre d'Aquila. It belonged to Darcey, who was the love of his life, and as he slid a gold band on her finger he whispered the words against her lips.

'I will love you for ever. My heart and soul are yours and there will never be any secrets between us.'

Darcey rested her hand on her stomach and smiled as she thought of the secret she would tell him later, when they were alone. She knew he would love their child unconditionally, as she would, and as they loved Rosa. But her heart belonged to Salvatore.

'I love you too,' she murmured and, reaching up on tiptoe, she kissed him.

* * * * *

A sneaky peek at next month...

MODERN™

INTERNATIONAL AFFAIRS, SEDUCTION & PASSION GUARANTEED

My wish list for next month's titles...

In stores from 15th November 2013:

❏ Defiant in the Desert – Sharon Kendrick

❏ Rumours on the Red Carpet – Carole Mortimer

❏ His Ultimate Prize – Maya Blake

❏ More than a Convenient Marriage? – Dani Collins

In stores from 6th December 2013:

❏ Not Just the Boss's Plaything – Caitlin Crews

❏ The Change in Di Navarra's Plan – Lynn Raye Harris

❏ The Prince She Never Knew – Kate Hewitt

❏ A Golden Betrayal – Barbara Dunlop

Available at WHSmith, Tesco, Asda, Eason, Amazon and Apple

Just can't wait?

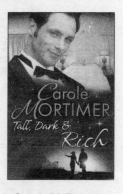

Come home this Christmas to Fiona Harper

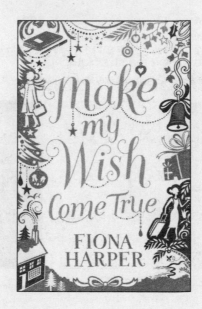

Make my Wish Come True

FIONA HARPER

From the author of *Kiss Me Under the Mistletoe* comes a Christmas tale of family and fun. Two sisters are ready to swap their Christmases—the busy super-mum, Juliet, getting the chance to escape it all on an exotic Christmas getaway, whilst her glamorous work-obsessed sister, Gemma, is plunged headfirst into the family Christmas she always thought she'd hate.

www.millsandboon.co.uk

Wrap up warm this winter with Sarah Morgan…

Sleigh Bells in the Snow

Kayla Green loves business and hates Christmas.

So when Jackson O'Neil invites her to Snow Crystal Resort to discuss their business proposal… the last thing she's expecting is to stay for Christmas dinner. As the snowflakes continue to fall, will the woman who doesn't believe in the magic of Christmas finally fall under its spell…?

4th October

www.millsandboon.co.uk/sarahmorgan

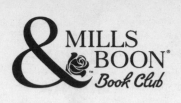 

Join the Mills & Boon Book Club

Subscribe to **Modern**™ today for 3, 6 or 12 months and you could **save over £40!**

We'll also treat you to these fabulous extras:

- 🌹 **FREE L'Occitane gift set worth £10**
- 🌹 **FREE home delivery**
- 🌹 **Rewards scheme, exclusive offers…and much more!**

Subscribe now and save over £40
www.millsandboon.co.uk/subscribeme